First published in 2017 by
Margaret River Press
PO Box 47
Witchcliffe
Western Australia 6286
www.margaretriverpress.com

Cataloguing-in-Publication data is available from the
National Library of Australia

ISBN: 978-0-6480275-0-8

Cover and text designed by Susan Miller
Typset in Adobe Caslon Pro, 11.75/16.45 pt
Edited by Ellen van Neerven
Printed in Australia by McPherson's Printing
Published by Margaret River Press, Western Australia

The paper in this book is FSC certified. FSC promotes
environmentally responsible, socially beneficial and
economically viable management of the world's forests.

Joiner Bay

& other stories

Edited by Ellen van Neerven

MARGARET RIVER
·PRESS·

The Margaret River Short Story Competition is sponsored by Margaret River Press and is now in its sixth year. The Southwest prize is sponsored by Edith Cowan University (Bunbury).

MARGARET RIVER
·PRESS·

Contents

Introduction

Reading short stories feeds the imagination. We are taken to new and surprising places quickly. Like putting on a VR headset but the effect is entirely achieved with words. I continue to be surprised by what can be achieved through good storytelling. The stories in this collection are very different, and in selecting the order, I have paid attention to this individual difference as well as the commonalities between stories. Somewhere in here, we find ourselves. Somewhere in here, we find each other.

We start with the 2nd prize-winning story, a speculative fiction story in 'Sheen' by Else

Fitzgerald. The 'sheens' are all that's left of our planet and they narrate the eaten landscape with their own languages and histories.

> It was so little I don't know how she seen it, but Roanie was often looking around us harder than anyone. She broke out of the line and went ploughing off into the deeper sand. I plunged after her, not wanting her to get sucked down while everything was still soft and unsettled from the storm. When I got to her she turned, a small bundle tucked in her arms. It was small and shaped like a human, but harder and it didn't move, made of a plastic not unlike our own skin. Its little eyes were stuck closed with sand but Roanie brushed them with her fingers and they blinked open. One didn't go up all the way, and underneath the eyes were still.

The othering of the familiar leaves the reader thinking of objects in their life, those that feel like a 'second skin' but void of life and meaning compared to the scale of environmental collapse and big-scale loss.

Highly commended 'Treacle Eyes' by Judyth Emanuel is also playful with language. The story follows two teenage twin sisters, Jani and Joanie, developing their separate identities in a sensory-filled world.

> Sometimes we lay us down. Twofold not much
> apart. Laid in the shade on the front lawn.
> Blowed dandelions. Knees warm bent. Summer
> day. This smell of damp grass. Must have rained
> before. Not heavy. Just dewdrops sprinkled.
> Jani sat in the sunny place. Jani a bit tipsy from
> cheap burgundy. I had a sip. Grimaced, 'Yuck.'
> Licked the tip of my finger. Held it up wet
> where. Seen which way the wind blew. Didn't
> want a screwed expression forever. Didn't want
> to get trapped.

As the sisters get older, the quieter, risk-averse Joanie fears their different paths will throw them apart. Not much is safe, and everything must be compromised.

'Oh, the Water' by Keren Heenan shows an Australian bush landscape where youth grow up and learn to manage their emotions. Our young male protagonist takes his dead father's fishing rod out to the river for the first time, during a downpour, and finds there are guides everywhere he looks.

And the neighbouring story 'Of the Water' by Jo Morrison also moves with this theme. This time the water is saltwater, and the narrator's lover is a keen surfer.

> Sometimes I think you were born of the water,
> a child of the sea. The clues were all there, in
> the dips and shadows of your body, the salt on
> your skin.

The story shows water in a particular Australian context can both give life and take it away, the danger is always real.

In Yvonne Edgren's highly commended story, 'Small Disturbances', a migrant grandmother of a minority language holds a fragile relationship with her Australian grandchildren. Liv, the oldest, is a keen thinker and decipher of her surrounds, in a large sprawling house, quiet except for the periodical sounds of the clock.

John Jenkins' 'Through A Latte Darkly' observes quick-witted coffee shop banter between two ex–AA members. Marco works as a barista and always serves coffee to his friend with an entertaining story and a few jokes. Their friendship feels to be the foundation of resisting addiction.

'A Single Life' by Marian Matta describes the trickiness for a loving couple of significant age difference as they descend into old(er) age. After

Nell's life-threatening fall, she begs Phillip to consider other options. Their life together may no longer be sustainable. The couple's tenderness and care for each other breathes light into the page.

'London via Paris and Rome' by Andreas Å Andersson is an original mix of sharehouse story and young backpacker story that explores the movements and relationships of the Union Street house's inhabitants, Mitch, Ron and Myra.

'Things to Come' by Charlotte Guest is a story about a long parting and illness. At the doctor's surgery, faced with the prospect of needing a carer for her senility, Olive is asked to think of someone to call. She thinks of her ex-partner, much in her mind but not in her life, ever since he told her forty years ago he could no longer have contact with her.

> She never could persuade him that it's okay
> to be unruly, that relationships are more
> innately liquid than he let them be. And yet she
> understood, like everyone understands, the need
> to alleviate pain.

A reunion under these circumstances moves with new and old language, repetition and rituals.

Winner of the Southwest prize, 'Harbour Lights' by Leslie Thiele moves from Western

Australian city and country and traces the pain in between spaces and adolescence and adulthood. Our narrator, Tanya, is confronted by her high-school attacker ten years on, now married to her new boss. Her home is threatened and her courage is tested; and her husband and child do not know of her silent struggle.

'Dependence Day' by Sophie McClelland is the story of a hundred-and-two-year-old man and his carer, his granddaughter. The wrestle for care and control of mind is present in his waking hours, and the all-present grief for his late wife.

'Ms Lovegrove' by Emily Paull describes the ambitions of a young university drama student, Nicole. Her life is changed by the arrival of a new tutor, Ms Lovegrove, a high-profile former star, who seems to be unimpressed by our narrator and her fellow students. To her surprise, Nicole is chosen to play the female lead in *A Streetcar Named Desire*, but Ms Lovegrove's method acting training begins to put our young character in an unsafe position.

The highly commended, 'Better Than the Farm' by Miriam Zolin explains to a Sydney newcomer the tips and traps of living in the monster city. Certain train stations are to be avoided, pedestrian etiquette is to be observed.

Step out of the train. Shuffle forward with
the mob. Follow them up the stairs and into
Greenwood Plaza or out onto the street. Try
not to think of sheep dogs and woolsheds. Stare
straight ahead and step aside for the ones on
urgent business.

'M' by Belinda McCormick charts two homeless
friends' journey, as they buckle in to survive the
winter. Desperate for food, M trades sexual favours
for hot noodle soup. M brings the food, while Gus
is watchdog, with an eye and ear for danger. But
things start getting precarious when the restaurant
owner begins to expect more from M, and Gus'
protection can not prepare them for change.

'All the Places You Have Been' by Erin
Courtney Kelly opens in the queue to see the corpse
flower, which blooms for only three days once every
thousand days, where Clare and her daughter are
hoping to catch a glimpse of it despite lining up
in the South Australian heat. The story moves to
explaining the meeting between Clare and her
daughter's father, which took place in a pub overseas.
He caught Clare's attention because of the way he
smelt 'like the forest'. Smell moves back into Clare's
life, in the overpowering stench of the corpse flower,

drawing her back to the unanswered past.

'Still Life with Dying Swan' by Gail Chrisfield shows the tender moments between a mother and daughter. Ali's mum is dying and she is trying to manage. She brings her mum to a health spa by a lake where swans flock. It's meant to be relaxing, but for Ali nothing is right.

'Joiner Bay' by Laura Elvery, the title story in the collection and winner of the 2017 Margaret River Short Story Competition, is set in a coastal community. The schoolboy narrator's best friend has just killed himself. But that's not why the boy is running. He can soak the whole bay up in his shoes if he tries. He has his dad giving him a ten for a PB. He and his dad both use the shared downstairs space as a gym.

> On the footpath winding up the hill, I dodge dozens of jackfruit that have split open. They are fat, fluorescent, mammalian. I see and hear the ocean. I try to steady my breath in through my nose and out my mouth.

When he slows down, he listens. And with the help of the school librarian, who recommends him books, he can start to make sense of his friend's sudden death.

These are beautiful, charming stories, top to bottom, stories I believe will enrich any reader.

Ellen van Neerven

Ellen van Neerven is a Mununjali woman from South East Queensland and the author of the award-winning short story collection *Heat and Light* (UQP, 2014) and the collection of poetry *Comfort Food* (UQP, 2016).

Sheen

Else Fitzgerald

Crefter was the first to rise, brushing the dust from his limbs. The air lay lank and heavy around us where we sat in a circle on the sand. The dead lead-grey sky was streaking with the red colour of day now, thick and unmoving overhead. The sun had not come up yet, but all the light that would come was here already. We stirred slowly; it was getting harder and harder as time went by, but we could never stop completely. Soon only Roanie was left lying down. Crefter poked at her with his foot, soft first, then a bit harder till he was nearly giving her a kicking. She came up slow, blinking those dark eyes I liked so much.

I was on a dreaming, Crefter, why'd you have to go on a kickin me?

We'd all heard about Roanie's dreaming many times, but it always stirred something in us. We moved around her, coming in close to hear it. Crefter stood apart, he didn't like the talking.

It was a flesh beast. It had four legs, and nice big eyes. I was a riding it, in my dreaming.

We all were quiet, trying to make a picture of the thing she talked about, but none of us could do it, except Thomas.

An equine. The humans kept them like us.

Thomas was the oldest one and he still knew things that the rest of us had forgotten or never even known. It was his remembering that made us crowd Roanie when she talked, because she dreamed true of things she didn't ever have known. I held my hands out to her and helped her to her feet, her limbs stretching in the dawn air. Roanie was the last one, the closest thing. Made in their image inside as well as out, much more than all the rest of us.

We walked all day while the big red sun bobbed just above the western horizon alongside us. Sometimes out of the murk ahead a tree would appear, a dry

skeleton of pale grey against the darker grey of
the sky. We saw them less and less though these
days, most of them had crumbled into dust by now.
Sometimes there were bones. Mostly of humans,
because they had lasted longest, but sometimes we
found other kinds. Thomas would try to remember
names of the things that used to own the bones, but
most times even he didn't know. We walked on. We
had our order now, the line of us alongside the sun.
Crefter went first, longing for the end. Then Grey
and Ren; smaller than the rest of us and identical
in every way. Then Roanie, then me. I liked to
walk behind her, so I could see the way she moved,
her body so like something real: fluid and alive.
Sometimes she would look at the sun, and I would
see the side of her face, soft in the red light. Thomas
came last behind. He was the slowest now.

When the sun went down we would have to
stop. None of us had the energy anymore to keep
going without the sun. It was old and didn't give
us as much as it had once. I tried to remember how
it had been, but the memory was only a brightness
now, and maybe the idea of something more yellow
than red. All the other things had gone away from
me. We were all settled on the sand now, and the
dark was on us proper. I could see their eyes open

in the black though. I crawled on the sand over to where Thomas was lying.

Could we have a fire tonight, Thomas? And maybe you could tell a story?

I could see his eyes looking up at the sky. He made a sound inside, a whirring noise.

I suppose we can. But it might be the last one. Do you still want to?

I nodded, crouching beside him in the gloom. He sat up and looked into the pack he carried. The one he'd saved till last was big, it would make a good burn. I helped with the tearing, I liked the way the paper made more of itself when it was scrunched. When we were done Thomas tented the cover on the top, and took his matches to the bottom of the stack. Thomas had never liked the burning of the books, but I knew he liked the light. Sheens love light. We have no real need of it, except the sun, but we are still drawn to it, longing to understand warmth. Everyone crowded in close, but not as close as me. I couldn't help but try to get right in to it; I had big melts on my hands and arms from wanting too much to touch it. Thomas put his hand on my shoulder. We were all quiet for the whoosh and flare of it, mesmerised by the colour.

After, when it was just the smoulder left, we sat

back to watch the bits of red flake off and float up into the dark. Thomas began to talk. Crefter got up and walked away from the circle.

The world is dead. Everyone who has come before you has died. You are the last, the last thing that moves.

Thomas's voice went on and up into the sky. I closed my eyes, back flat against the cold sand. I lay still for a long time, but it wasn't really. How long had it been? I used to try and remember how many nights and days had passed, but after so long I forgot, and there didn't seem to be any reason to keep on at it.

I sat up. The night was at the darkest, and I was slow in the moving. I moved across the sand to where Crefter sat. He didn't look at me, and I thought he might like for me to go away. I didn't though.

I'm sorry about the fire, Crefter.

I meant sorry about the story. I knew Crefter didn't like it when Thomas told stories about Before. Crefter was the leader; it was his wanting that made us all walk every day. All Crefter wanted was a forgetting, an end. We followed him because it was in us to obey, and there was nothing else we could do.

**

The morning came a sickly colour, the sky all
browny and mean-looking. By afternoon, a wind was
skirling over the sand, getting fiercer. The ground
started shifting and the air was thick with dust. We
joined hands in a big link. Ren and Grey wanted
to stop, but Crefter dragged on. Stopping was bad
because the sand could bury you real quick if you
were still, and then you'd be stuck down underneath,
hoping someone would come and dig you out.
More like you'd have to wait till the next big wind
unburied you, and that could be a long time. I liked
the wind storms because after sometimes you'd find
the desert had spat up all kind of things. Maybe we
would find more things to burn.

Finally the wind blew itself out and the air
cleared. All the hills and bumps in the land had
moved around, but we could still tell the way by
walking on next to the sun. It was so little I don't
know how she seen it, but Roanie was often looking
around us harder than anyone. She broke out of the
line and went ploughing off into the deeper sand.
I plunged after her, not wanting her to get sucked
down while everything was still soft and unsettled
from the storm. When I got to her she turned,
a small bundle tucked in her arms. It was small

and shaped like a human, but harder and it didn't move, made of a plastic not unlike our own skin. Its little eyes were stuck closed with sand but Roanie brushed them with her fingers and they blinked open. One didn't go up all the way, and underneath the eyes were still. She carried it back to the line and I followed. The others crowded round to have a look. Grey poked at it with a finger, but Thomas just looked and then said,

It's only a doll, Roanie.

We all looked at him.

A toy. Some small human's thing for playing.

I didn't know the words he was saying, but I saw the look on Roanie's little face. She was all lit like a shining kind of thing.

Late, late. The nights got so black now, and they felt endless. Above me the sky was bottomless, a depth that went on and on. The stars had mostly burned out long ago, the dead light leftover, travelling through space. I wondered if the last humans were up there somewhere, on their arks. My thoughts fell into that infinite blackness, I lost contact with the world around me. A world which contained nothing, was empty but for my fellow masheens clicking their limbs in the dark. I went up into the night. The dream of the end was up there somewhere, the hope of a time when everything, at last, might finally stop. The sadness crept in me, that idea of a feeling they'd given me long ago. In the night I cursed those humans for their selfishness. For leaving us behind, to go on and on indefinitely, while the world around us withered and finally died, with just the sun slowly burning out. So slowly.

Away in the black I heard voices and I crawled toward the noise. Thomas and Crefter were talking, invisible in the night. I knew the talk, the same words as always.

Why should we keep going, Crefter?

Because I'm tired. I want to turn Off.

Maybe there is no way.

Thomas's voice was desolate, slapping flatly against the night.

They would not do that to us. There must be a way.

You don't know them like I did, Crefter. They gave no thought to us.

I heard it in Thomas's voice too, the thing we shouldn't know but did. A human thing, left over long after all of them were gone, the sadness the last thing of all. Crefter was quiet a long time but finally when I thought the silence would go on till morning he spoke.

We have nothing else to do.

I lay on the cold sand, a prisoner of my unchanging wakefulness. I heard, dimly, Crefter stomp away. Thomas settled on the ground near me, his insides grinding.

Tell me again about the children, Thomas.

Flesh from flesh, slithering from the body into the air. The first breath, the heart beating wildly under the light. The newborn human became something else in time. What I wished for the most was change, the one thing we could never do.

The days went on. Crefter pushed us further, we walked until our feet began to wear away. Thomas was quiet. Roanie cradled the doll in her arms, and a memory flickered in me. Something began to bloom in Roanie that should never have been able to be there. I knew she was different from me, had been made for a different purpose. I could only remember the factory, the unending and unchanging work where I stood in line and connected wiring, making more of myself. And then the dark years in the storage container after my decommissioning. Until the world broke, and the storms and the seas destroyed everything they had built, leaving us behind in the rubble.

In the evening we stopped. I found her behind the dunes. The others were off sitting in the last of the sunlight, but I'd come looking for her. She had the doll close against her chest, rocking it gently back and forth. I came up to her. She was humming quietly, a tune I didn't know.

In the factory, they said that was for children, something the mothers would sing. I always wanted one for myself.

Her voice ached. She laid the doll aside. I watched while she unwrapped the tattered cloth that covered her; saw the churning metal of her parts underneath. She looked up at me and I saw green in her eyes, that forgotten colour I never thought to see again.

I've seen you looking at me.

She was purring nearly, laid out before me. I wanted so badly, but the anatomy of me would not allow it. She looked long in my eyes, and I saw the worst kind of thing there: a hopeless wishing for things that would never be real for us. Made in their image, but made all the same.

I don't want to go on anymore.

Her voice was dead now, her eyes gone dark. I touched her face one time, like I'd been wanting for so long. Then I reached around behind me and picked up the biggest rock I could find.

I did Crefter next, and the joy in him made the bad of it less for me. He came apart under the stone. I saw the light go out of him, felt him go still. I turned to the others.

Thomas was last. We sat for a minute amongst the wreckage of the others, looking out over the sand. I gripped his hand tight, and he looked long in my face, eyes full of hope. I felt the loneliness rear up in me, but I knew I had to do this last thing for my friend.

Are you ready, Thomas?

He nodded.

What will you do?

I looked up at the sky darkening above us, the sun hanging heavy above the horizon, the vast dust-coloured land stretching around us.

I'll just wait.

He smiled at me, and closed his eyes.

Treacle Eyes

Judyth Emanuel

Sometimes we lay us down. Twofold not much apart. Laid in the shade on the front lawn. Blowed dandelions. Knees warm bent. Summer day. This smell of damp grass. Must have rained before. Not heavy. Just dewdrops sprinkled. Jani sat in the sunny place. Jani a bit tipsy from cheap burgundy. I had a sip.

Grimaced.

'Yuck.'

Licked the tip of my finger. Held it up wet where. Seen which way the wind blew. Didn't want a screwed expression forever. Didn't want to get trapped.

Jani gazed at our bright sun. Mind the burn. Shine reaching her. But I covered my face hate the brightness. Wondered. When what was the future? Wouldn't be maybe a suffered. But thought a sun imagined extraordinary times ahead. That's what suns did above.

Then Jani shouted, 'Joanie, I'm CRAZY as.'

She never said what.

Here in Forestville. Way way out. Twins Jani and Joanie. Seventeen freckled almost identical. I was fatter. Podge porridge. We throbbed giggles. Get us. So desperate for rose-coloured glasses, go-go boots, corduroy mini-skirts. Girls growing cheeky up. Fast hormones busted. Jani made the V-sign. Far Out. Somehow. Said in unison,

'Peace. Ban The Bomb. Yep, far out, man.'

Groovy girls but supposed to be gooder than good. Even on the inside. I was. But not Jani. She was lovely on the inside. On the outside, a wild girl. Much braver than the wallflower. Jani sniffed my armpits,

'You got B.O.'

'Meanie, get me some roll-on.'

Every day I watched brain dead. Boggled goggled *Gidget* on telly. TV Gidget girl said, 'Wait just a dingy minute. Life is a gas.' Oh her dimples dreamed of Moondoggy. Life should be a gas. Might not be a gas. Wondered again. So. Every morning I drank black coffee. Nescafé instant sweetened with heaped teaspoons of sugar. Felt sophisticated. Us dingy girls so sugary loved.

Jani said, 'You're a sweet tooth, Joanie.'

Both of us barefoot in polyester nightgowns. Nylon lace itched. Her breasts bigger under ruffles. High neckline for me no cleavage.

'Got no boobs,' I said.

'Phooey. You're nuts, Joanie.'

She saw more than I ever could. She said, 'Fuck the world. Jeezus Gawd almighty.' So daredevil to talk shit blasphemy.

'Shush, that's rude swears.'

She beamed, 'Fuck. You say it. Go on ...'

Hours we spent in the bedroom. Sometimes bored. She was. Single beds, side-by-side, rosy chenille bedspreads. Mine with hospital corners. Hers rumpled. This monotony so what.

And I kept a diary. 'Don't look, nosy parker.'

Cupped left hand. Hid the nonsense. Scribbled with a Bic biro. Drew paisley shapes. Pencilled stick figures with pulsating hearts floating up from flat chests. In composition book. Blue lines. Same blue as our eyes. I wrote silly sloping neat. Blue ink. *PRIVATE. Thoughts during 1978. So far this year I have been very very happy. But then ...* But then what?

Watched Jani blow smoke rings out the window so Mum wouldn't know. She pressed thumb tacks into pink cotton cloth. Ouch prickly. Sickly. Little skirt attached it to the dressing table daggy. Jani sat at it. Squinted at reflection. My chin on her shoulder. Look at us. Doubled. Same but not the same. The plain and the dazzle. Then she crimped her hair with metal butterfly clips. I helped. Every strand sprang from her scalp in great blonde waves.

'Wow,' I said, 'That looks gorgeous.'

Jani twirled in front of the mirror. 'Am I foxy or what?'

Butterfly clips had sharp teeth. Left my hair lank. Didn't bleach like hers. Her hair done. Get ready to.

'Make me up,' she said.

I plastered gobs of sparkly eye shadow on her eyelids. Coated her fair lashes with mascara copying Twiggy. Only more gaudier. Now me. Painted my eyelids blue. Too blue. Trashy. Eyelashes black brittle. Looked stupid ha. Cheap that stuff.

'Prostitutes,' screamed Mum at the sight of us. 'What's that black junk round yer eyes?' Ignorant woman never heard of mascara. Smacked *me* in the head. Not Jani.

Then tears. Then. Gave up on happiness. Did this for no reason. Knew life was sad, before it got sad. Spilled a lot of sobs dissolving mascara. Black tears running down my freckles. Blinked. Looked like treacle.

'Treacle eyes,' I told Jani.

'What the fuck is treacle?'

'Sweet syrup,' I said. 'Chocolate honey only richer darker goop.'

'Don't cry, Joanie, it can't be that bad.'

But it was. I didn't understand why. Wasn't right to be goodie two shoes. The introverted. Melancholic that's what terrible. Settled for one-dimensional life sort of like world map glued to the surface of my little teak desk. Countries coloured wishy-washy pastels. Pale oceans here and there. Where to go. Jani shoved me, not hard but gentle.

'Let's go out.'

'Mum says we're not allowed.'

'Don't care.' Jani gadded about, did what she wanted. Every Saturday night snuck out to pool halls, pinball machines, pimply boys combed over, kids mucking around. She wore vintage dresses, torn T-shirts. She towered in turquoise laced-up platform boots, eight inches high. From this towering height called, 'See ya later, alligator.'

'Be careful,' I said.

Her yellow hair springing. Jani walked to the bus stop. Past rockeries bordering plump shrubs in front gardens of brick homes hiding secret lives bending a single slat of venetian blinds. Peered at blonde. Jani got past all that. Waited for the bus on Warringah Road. Heads turned. Traffic slowed. The usual breezes blew easy. Crimson satin dress swirled around her slender frame. Showed skinny legs. Those brilliant boots. Streak of a figure. Shocked hair. Like a pink palm tree on which the bright sun shone. And even gone, I sensed her there like a whisper in the room.

A year later, her life spiralled. Thought it fashionable to have morbid ideas.

'Joanie, I won't see twenty-five. You'll find me slumped in an alleyway. Die pretty, that's what they say.'

I felt scared. 'What idiot says that? Who?'

'Oh you know. Some rock band.'

And she sang her favourite song. *Take a walk on the wild side* ... Which she did with robber boyfriend. Mick deadhead doper. Sold some. Mick mainline tripper gave Jani heroin, LSD, hepatitis. Mick drove the getaway van not fast enough. Got two years in prison. Jani drifted high for a while.

I chose a quiet path. Why not. Most women read *The Female Eunuch*. I did too. But I kind of missed the point. Didn't have the whole cheeky arse, long legs, sexy voice, market value. I did finally have nice tits though. I married Jesus freak Rodney. *If you're happy and you know it clap your hands.* A golden halo of curls circled his head. Puffy hair really. And wire-rimmed spectacles gave him a nerdy air. Hard to look him in the eye. His beard hid narrow moist lips. I ducked when he tried to kiss me. Ugh, I thought, not that.

Then Jani on the doorstep. Needed a place to crash. Rodney frowned. Shook his puffed head.

And the obedient wife betrayed windswept girl.

'It's okay,' Jani said. Huddled in an inner city squat. Her wistful voice, 'Do ya love him, Joanie?'

Course I didn't. Cripes. Girls couldn't survive what real love was. And I thought love wasn't anything. Still Rodney's sperm wriggled up my unmentionable. Collided with whatever inside this ripe young womb. Seed now planted. The rest of our lives. Never naked in bed again. Angry the

bed. Made V-sign in reverse. Now every morning.
Thought about eating sand. Day after day. Retched.
Gazed at blank walls. Wallflowered.

Jani stuck needles in her veins. Sometimes she
dropped acid, dropped everything, dropped out,
dropped by. 'Are ya happy, Joanie?'

'Yeah. Not really.' Just so glad to see her.

'Give us a hug.'

How bone thin she was. I patted concealer onto
the shadows under her hollow eyes. Head rested on
my belly. Listened to the swell. Laughed swelled, 'I
can feel it move.'

I said, 'I think it's a baby.'

The baby born a month later. Jani still sick
from hepatitis. Weighed five stone. Came to visit
me. Shadow of herself. At the front desk of the
maternity ward, the nurse told her, 'You're not
allowed in here.'

Baby Matty I named him. Rodney chanted, 'Praise
the Lord.'

'Yes,' I said, 'You do that.'

And stopped eating meat. Blamed the placenta.
Nobody showed me. Slippery red thing slipped
away. Night and day. I breastfed with two cracked
nipples. What did they diagnose it. Never mind. The

pain. It hurt. Matty wailed. Pulled away from me. His head like a beetroot yanked from the soil. I tried my best. Breast refusal, the experts called it. Nursing strike. Fussy baby. Both of us on edge. *The Womanly Art of Breastfeeding* advised: 'Gently rock your baby.' Every day night, I rocked Matty. All perfection cherub smelling of baby lotion rubbed in. But he rejected bursting breasts as if he knew. The sorrow embedded. Howled hungry at defective mother. Beetroot baby swaddled in bunny rugs. I sprinkled Johnson's baby powder over his nappy rash. 'Go to sleep,' I said. And it took a long time.

After midnight. More of a nightmare. Bell rang loud as a fire alarm. Four o'clock on a Sunday morning. The telephone at that hour. 'Please don't wake the baby.' Breasts ached. Hard as rockmelons. Almost exploded from rejected milk. Phone kept ringing. What sticky grit eyes half-opened. Rodney switched on the bedside lamp. He searched for his glasses. He answered the phone. Kept voice muffled into mouthpiece. Closed my eyes too tired to think something could be wrong. Relieved Matty hadn't woken. Heard a click. Rodney quietly replaced the receiver. He leaned over. Took my hand.

'Joanie. Your mother rang. Just now.'

I groaned. Heat in my head. Should bang it on

the pillow. Mum. Prayed on her knees. *Life will break you.* Broke me didn't speak to her for years. Made me feel guilty about nothing. I froze stiff. Remembered Mum. Hemmed in by dishrags. How she boiled sweet sour sauce with tinned pineapple. Slathered the vileness on lamb chops. Smile radiated joyful Christian. But her eyes sneaky with sweet and sour. Why she phoned forcing me awake.

Rodney said, 'Your mother told me Jani met a boy at a party last night. He offered her a ride home in his MG convertible.' Rodney began crying small sniffs. 'Dear God, it's difficult.'

Stopped breathing. Bothered what he meant. I pulled my hand away. 'What is. Tell me.'

The dim light dawned. Rodney wiped his eyes. 'The boy was drunk. He lost control of the car. Jani died in the accident.'

I sat bolt upright. As if someone pushed me hard from behind. My heart thudded *slippery road, sharp bend*. Skid marks blazed through me. Opened my mouth to scream. Terrible soft sound came out and out and out ribbon pulled from throat. Sick noise of. Pure anguish. Soundless sobbed. Doubled over *drunk driver, no seat belt* punched me in the stomach, *sports car, top down*. Sweet Jesus took one second, felt the floor gone. Great blonde waves disappeared.

Rag doll thrown down dead end. Killed. Instantly.
That candle burning in the bloody wind. Fizzed
out. Never again the girl I was. Air trapped tight in
neck. And then I hit Rodney. I whacked him hard
across the face. Threw Bible at him. Bashed Bible.
Tore pages screaming,

'She wanted to live with us but you wouldn't
let her.'

He shrank to the size of the red welt on his
cheek. 'Neither did you.'

'That's a lie.'

Torture paced for hours. Slopped tears hell.
Dried eyes and rang my mother back. Hardly made
sense.

'Was watching *Homicide*,' she said. 'Police
officers knocked at the door. Had to go—had
to find. Emergency on my own. Her teeth were
shattered.'

'Don't tell me,' I said slamming the phone
down.

Rodney sank in our quicksand bed. Balls
peeping from a split in his flannel pyjama pants.
Rodney prayed to spiteful God. Took her from
me. No longer believed in. Rodney reduced to. His
bleating. 'I don't know what to do.'

I said, 'Leave me alone.'

**

When did I see her? Last week at The Sad Clown
café. I lent her twenty quid. She grinned showing
gaps. Last week. Smiley faces. Last week, she was. A
living, breathing girl. Stick figure. What did I say?

'Lend me your lippy, mine's run out.'

'Mine too,' she replied. 'What about some
mascara? I got a brand new tube.' She scrabbled
around in her suede bag stitched with long fringing.
The ripped lining useful for shoplifting.

'Here ya go. Stole it from Woolies last week.'

That last week of the last week. And now.

The baby woke up. Crying. Damn. I nursed. Blue
eyes looking up at me. Blue same as ours. Tears fell
on his tears. Still he refused broken nipples. Oh
what had Jesus Christ done to us. Hating God be
fucked. I hunched over the washbasin. I ran the
hot tap until the bathroom mirror fogged. The red
swollen face of a girl obliterated. Made the V-sign.
Then forefinger scrawled FUCK THE WORLD
on the misted glass. Somehow my fault this agony
soap wouldn't wash. Squeezed my breast. Milk
spurted in a thin stream down the plughole. Should
have saved all that lost milk. Stored it chilled.
Somewhere safe. Could have rescued Jani. Rocked

her gently. Her wounds. Her wasted body. Wan face. Wicked laugh.

**

I slept, didn't know how. Woke to dazzling sunlight. Not fair. This betrayal, hating brightness. This day she could never see. Cruel suns hung low on the skyline. Impression of two suns in the sky. Light deflected by crystals in the clouds and hey presto twin suns appeared. Learned this at school in science class. Stared blind at those double suns. God help me. Suns might stay in full view forever. Made earth too bright. Two shitty bugger bastard suns too many. Too late for Jani in the dark of dark.

Her gone said, *Don't stand by my grave and weep.* But I did. That bedraggled group. Rodney, my mother, Matty and me weeping at Jani's funeral. I wept at miserable little shrine my mother created beside the simple casket. Jani's hippy beads strung between two lit candles. Swinging just a fraction. A lace handkerchief draped around a framed photograph. Jani wearing flared jeans ripped at the knees. Defiant eyes lined with blue eyeliner. The blue of our eyes. Leggy lashes disembodied above chalky lips. Cheekbones scattered with freckles once daubed with lemon juice. *So far this year I have been very very happy. But then …*

Her screw the universe voice, 'Stop that crying, treacle eyes.'

Rodney nudged me. Slipped a wad of tissues into my pocket. I forgot to wear sunglasses. I must look awful. *You're awful, Joanie.* Smudged eyes exposed. Jani's stolen mascara *Maybelline, got it on sale, only $4.99, her joke, yeah pull the other one.* Black tears ran down my cheeks. *Don't cry, treacle eyes, it can't be that bad.* My panda face. Same as Jani's face. But much sadder. Grief filled a girl right up before the funeral ended. I thought, *get it out of me.* Grief drained from my tongue, lungs, uterus. Leaked from the hole where the baby came out. The hole I never touched.

I glanced at Matty in my arms. Sweet there and real. Rodney bowed his head. His hair fastened in a wretched little rat's tail. If I had a pair of scissors, I might cut it off. This severing. Not love. He sang the last hymn. 'Amazing Grace, I once was lost.'

Jani got lost. Half of myself knew what to do. Still lost.

'Was blind but now I see.'

So walk away, God said. I had to walk away. And if. I just melted away. Nobody would notice.

'When we've been there ten thousand years.'
Didn't sing the last hymn. 'Bright shining as the sun.'

I started to go. To get away. Stealthily. Should
I run?

'We've no less days.'

Took a step backwards. A few more steps. Slow.
Glacial. Treacle. This thick substance a barrier. Get
through it. And I almost did. But Rodney reached
across and grabbed my arm. He turned to me. His
glasses gleamed, 'Shall be forever mine.'

Oh, the Water

Keren Heenan

We're only a few ks away but the rain is getting heavy now. We shelter under a big old pine tree and share Thommo's chips. Wet fingers make them soggy, and they've been scrunched in his pocket so they're all crumby now. Then through the white haze of the rain we see a car coming along the road and I race out to flag it down.

It's some old guy in a beaten up truck with a pile of junk in the back. He skids to a halt on his bald tyres and the windscreen wipers are thrashing about like crazy. He pushes open the passenger door and we throw the fishing gear in the back and tumble in like a couple of wet dogs. He puts the heater on and soon enough it's nice and cosy with the three of us crammed in on the bench seat, our breath fogging up the windows and steam starting to rise off our wet clothes. 'Just a sun-shower,' he says. He has the radio on and he starts singing away to a song like we're not even there: 'Oh, the water, oh-oh the water, hope it don't rain all day.'

Me and Thommo look at one another and grin, and on the next chorus we both chime in: 'Oh the water ...' and the old guy shows us his rotten teeth in a big chuckle, and before long we're hollering the chorus and can't even hear the music. When it finishes, he says, 'Ah, Van the Man. Good song that,' and he slaps the wheel and starts at the chorus again. But we've had enough of singing and we leave him to it. I rub my hand over the fogged up window and look out at the hills, the sheep with their heads down in a mournful packed-in huddle.

The rain's easing off up ahead and by the time we reach town, the sun's out again and the sky's blue enough to make you wonder where all that rain came from. The old guy, whose name is Joe, *but you can call me Fish*, stops the truck at the crossroads and says, 'Where you young fellas off to anyway?'

'We're just going home now.'

'Yeah, we've been out fishing.'

'Didja get any?'

We look at each other and Thommo says, 'Nothing we could bring home. All too small.'

'Ah, I see. Now if youse want a real good fishing spot,' he taps his nose, and I'm never sure when people do that what it means. I look at Thommo and his face tells me he doesn't know either.

'Ya know?' Joe, or Fish, says, and we both wait for him to tell us more. 'Well,' he says, patting the seat, 'youse can just stay put, I'm goin' past it, just down the road a bit.' And before we answer, or even look at each other, he's turned right, out of town. I look at Thommo and he shrugs, and soon we're bouncing along again, the junk shifting around in the back of the truck because he hasn't tied anything down. A couple of ks out the road he turns down a gravel track. 'Just a bit further,' he says, leaning over the steering wheel so he can see the pot holes coming up. He's weaving and dodging and manages not to hit any.

He pulls up when the track disappears into scrub leaving just a thin path where all the grass has been flattened down. He lifts one finger from the steering wheel and points to the path. 'Straight ahead, boys. Best little fishing spot this side o' the black stump. Don't go spreading it around though,'

and he taps his nose again. Thommo and me nod,
like partners in a top secret mission. Fish is staring
straight ahead, then he says, 'Ya know what? I'll
come with youse. I fancy a bit of fish for dinner.'

I'm starting to feel a bit embarrassed because
we're not very good at fishing. In fact, today was
the first day we've been out. My dad's rod has hung
in the shed since he died and it was my mum who
said I should give it a run. 'Why don't you and
James take the fishing gear out, see if you can catch
anything. Your father would've loved to see it put
to use.' Thommo had his dad's rod, so he was eager
to give it a go. But if old Fish is as good at fishing
as his name says, then he'll think we're a couple of
losers. We nearly caught a couple of good ones this
morning, but I don't think Thommo put the bait
on properly. As soon as we felt a tug and went to
pull them in, there was nothing there. We couldn't
even catch the little ones we told Fish about. If he
comes with us we're going to have to own up to not
knowing jack shit about fishing.

Thommo says okay to Fish, real confident like,
but then he turns to me and pulls one of his mock-
horror faces. Anyway, I figure it can't be all bad,
at least we might learn something about fishing.
I never went out with my dad much; I always had

33

footy on Saturdays, and school holidays I never wanted to waste sitting on some river bank waiting for a fish. I thought fishing was a fairly boring thing to do but it wasn't too bad with Thommo this morning. We just talked crap and laughed and skipped stones if nothing was biting. Not that I can skip stones, but Thommo's old man taught him and he tried to teach me. The fish all pissed off after that anyway and we figured we may as well call it a day—or a morning at least. Now here we are getting a second go at it all in one day.

Fish's door sticks a bit but he finally shoves it open. He gets out and takes a big plastic tub from the back of the truck. 'Haven't got me rod, but I can use one of you boys'?'

I shove my rod forward. 'Yeah, sure, here, use mine,' and Fish puts his hand up and ushers me and my rod down the path in front of him.

'No water here Sonny-me-lad, wait'll we get there. And watch out for snakes.'

I hadn't thought about snakes, with the rain and all, but the sun's out now and it's getting heated up again. It occurs to me as we're walking down the path, heads swinging looking for snakes, that old Fish might be some sort of weirdo, luring us down

a lonely path just to bludgeon us and toss our bodies
in the river. And I think of my mum and how she'd
feel hearing the news, and how she'd hate herself
for saying to take the fishing rod out, and then how
she'd feel having no-one—not my dad, not me—
no-one to get spiders out of the bathroom, or open
tight lids, and lift heavy stuff when her back's sore.
I think I can feel Fish's eyes boring into the back of
my head, and I'm feeling so bad for my mum now
that I swing around to check what he's doing. Just
as I turn I hear a clattering noise and Fish lurches
at me with this look on his face like he's a madman,
and he lifts me up. I start to thrash about and then
I can see Fish isn't looking at me, he's looking at the
ground. And a long black tail disappearing into the
scrub. He puts me down then and picks up the tub
that he dropped to grab me. He says, 'I toldja, keep
your eyes peeled. You were a coupla inches away
from steppin' on 'im.'

'Shit!' Thommo's still staring at the spot where
the snake disappeared, as if it's still there, rearing up
at us, fangs ready to sink into my leg. Fish reaches
out and pushes me in behind him on the path and
I'm worried there's another one. But he's just taking
the lead, seeing as how I wasn't very good at being
in front. We keep walking, heads swinging left and

right again. And this time I don't get distracted from the job. 'Blue-bellied black,' Fish says, his head bobbing about on his beanpole neck. 'Pretty damn ven'mous, if ya don't get help real quick. Not like a copperhead though, or the brown, or the tiger. The taipan, now you'd be dead as a doornail that one gotcha.'

I'm imagining them coming at us from all sides now, and I wish we were back in the truck, dodging pot holes or singing that water song at the top of our lungs. I take a look over my shoulder at Thommo and his eyes are popping out too but he's looking all over the place, in front of him and behind and left and right. When I turn around again I can see the river in front of us, and there's a cleared space on the bank with some rocks where we can sit without worrying about snakes.

'Here we go,' Fish says, and puts the tub down. It's a big tub and I reckon he must think we're some big-shot fishermen, and I don't want to let him down, not after he's shown us his favourite spot and all. And saved me from that black snake. 'Where's ya bait? he says and Thommo gives him the worms. We'd spent ages in the compost plucking out the fattest ones. 'Not much,' he says. 'Never mind. It'll do.'

We both look really close when he's putting the worm on the hook. He uses his thumbnail to cut one in half, and I feel a bit squirmy watching the quick slice of his nail. I wonder if they can feel anything. You can see their muscles working, pulling them along in waves, pretty neat really. But Fish isn't admiring their movements, he just pushes the hook through the worm's body and leaves the tail bit wriggling around for the fish to see and get excited about.

'Should be a whole lotta worms in a wriggling mess, but this'll do.' He casts my line into the river all smooth like, with a nice little plop into the water. 'Jus' let the bait sink a bit, wait … Wait,' he says as if it's my hands on the rod not his. His eyes are on the water. 'Let it settle,' then his hands jerk and I think he's caught something already. 'Bring it up again, towards the middle there. Then nice and slow like, bring it up to the top a bit. Gets the little fishy interested 'cos he thinks there's some tasty little morsel gettin' away,' and he gives a low chuckle. He gives the rod to me, like he's done the hard stuff that he knows we're probably crap at, then he repeats the whole thing with Thommo. And we stand there grinning at each other, holding our rods like we've done this loads of times before.

Fish sits on a rock and rolls a cigarette then leans back blowing smoke over his shoulder like he doesn't want to pollute the river, or us, which I think is pretty nice of him. Instead of ashing his cigarette on the ground he taps it with one finger onto his knee and then rubs the palm of his hand over it, rubbing the ash into his trousers. He's humming the song— *oh, the water*—soft and light like he's calling in the fish to our hooks. Sun's out now so the shadows of trees are falling over the water. One tree's toppled over, roots stretched up and out like it's in shock from the light. Branches dip in the water and mini whirlpools spin around them. The water is making that soft low gurgle like it's all safe and warm and we're on a picnic on the bank. But I imagine falling in when the water's wild and churning up mud and silt from the bottom, chunks of wood and rocks swirling by, and all that dirty brown water in my nose and mouth. And then the branch in front of me like a lifeline and I'd grab onto it and hold on tight while the rest of my body floats out behind me, shirt spread like a kite and me just another piece of river junk to be carried away topsy-turvy downstream. But then old Fish would be there on the trunk, leaning down to me with his hand out and I'd grab it with my free hand and he'd pull me up.

But I'm not in the river. I'm safe on the bank and the water isn't swirly, it's gentle and just gurgling along. And Fish is beside me on his rock, smoking his cigarette and humming his song. It's peaceful in the sun with all the river noises, the day passing by in the clouds, the water running like a tap that's left on but just a gentle stream. Things plop in the water, and a couple of dragonflies chase in and out of the leaves on the tree arched over the river. And I'm wondering what it would've been like here with my dad. I imagine telling him about it, this great little spot on the river, *best ever fishing spot*, even though we haven't caught anything yet. And just as I think that, I feel a niggle on the line, just a little jerk like something's testing it out, and Fish is right there beside me like he was waiting and watching too. 'Now take it easy, lad.'

I can feel the weight of the fish on the line, and I'm thinking it must be pretty big. Or it's a gumboot or some other river crap. I know Thommo's looking so I'm hoping it's a big one.

When it comes up and out of the water, it's not a gumboot, it's a fish. Not gigantic but a good-sized one. I can see Thommo's jealous. But before I can even get it off the hook, Thommo's making noises and jumping around like he's got a whale on his line.

When he reels it in it's the same size as mine and we're both grinning away and Fish is chuckling and loading up our hooks again, and I'm thinking this fishing caper is pretty easy.

Later, when I look up I can see the sun is starting to sink. On the opposite bank the trees' lacy leaves are like a tattoo on the sky. Fish puts the top on the plastic tub and says, 'Come on then. I'd better git you fellas home.' It's only then that I realise he didn't use my rod, or Thommo's. He just put the bait on for us, showed us how to cast out. Still, I reckon we'd better give him some fish. There's plenty there.

When I get home, my mum is so impressed with the haul she doesn't even tell me off for being late. Instead, when I tell her about old Fish and how he took us to his secret spot and showed us how to put the bait on and everything, she says, 'Joe Ling, yes, your dad used to talk about him. Nice old fellow. A bit eccentric. Lives out past the lagoon in an old shack, no telephone, no mod cons.' I'm not sure what *eccentric* means, but it's the sort of word that seems to suit him so I don't ask. 'He used to take your dad to that *secret spot*,' she smiles. And I can imagine him and Dad sitting there on the rocks, waiting for the fish to bite, the quiet river around them and the lazy dragonflies and the sun sinking down. I'm still holding onto the rod and me and Mum both look at it like it's my dad standing there between us. We look at each other then she says, 'Go and pop it in your room. It's yours now,' and she runs her fingers through my hair.

In my room I lean the rod against the wall. I'm thinking that I might get Thommo to come with me out past the lagoon one day to try and find Fish's place.

We get a lot of rain over the next couple of days. Me and Thommo had great plans for the holidays but we haven't seen each other since fishing. Then finally, the day cracks open like an egg, all yellow sun and blue sky. I'm lying in bed but I can feel the sun through the window.

Out in the kitchen Mum is sitting at the table drinking tea and reading the paper. I get myself some toast and start thinking about the day. My mum makes a noise like she's hurt herself or something. She looks up at me, one hand spread out on the paper and her mouth open, and I know she's read some bad news. She always takes it hard, even though she doesn't know the people. She pats the paper a couple of times. And then she tells me.

Apparently he'd had a bit to drink, was on

his way home night before last, in his old truck, probably with all the junk still in the back, and those bald tyres, that door that doesn't open properly. He skidded on the gravel and ended up in the lagoon. It's not deep, but he couldn't get out of the truck. Someone found him next morning.

And I'm thinking the song, mouthing the words but no sound comes out. I make the toast and spread the butter slowly, watching the yellow blobs melt away. The song rolls on, like it's on a loop, through my head.

Of the Water

Jo Morrison

I'm standing cold in the sand, trying to see Rottnest Island through the sky's swathes of grey. My face is slick with tears that taste of you. No-one can tell me why the intensity of my grief—the savagery of it, the way it has me by the throat—isn't enough to bring you back.

Sometimes I think you were born of the water, a child of the sea. The clues were all there, in the dips and shadows of your body, the salt on your skin.

First time you saw me, I was lying on the floor of our rehearsal space, timber boards cool beneath me. I was to be your Echo and you my Narcissus, to spurn me, reduce me to a bodiless state, no more than reflected sounds in a cave.

I'd arrived early and found the room empty,
a silent space waiting for me, inviting me to shut
my eyes, just for a minute. I closed the door and
lay down in a darkness so dense I could barely see
my hands held above my head. I could have been
anywhere, anytime, breathing in the hush and
breathing it out again. Until voices intruded on the
soundscape, growing louder, coming closer. Light
seared into the room when you opened the door,
made me lift my hand to shield my eyes. I must've
looked a strange waif, there on the floor.

Sometimes I think if I can just pick out these
details, map them out with enough precision, then
you'll materialise here in front of me, just as you
were. The way your left eyebrow kinked up at the
edge, and that scar near your ear ... I wanted to
touch it even then, to let my fingers slide down the
groove behind your jaw and slip round under the
collar of your coat.

I stood up, brushing the fine dust off the backs
of my legs, and I'm sure I smiled because how could
I not have smiled on first seeing you, your lovely
face, haloed by the light? A face I felt I knew, as
though I'd run a finger along each line around your
eyes already.

Lara turned on more lights and the boundless darkness became a walled room, not very big, only five rows of seats running along three walls. She got us to help her drag those two benches on to the stage. One to represent the seats in a train, the other a bench at the station. Remember?

You look at your watch, confused. I follow you as you walk along the platform to press the information button. A disembodied voice intones: 'Your next train departs in seventeen minutes.'

    'Idiot,' you mutter.

    Softly, I echo you: 'Idiot.'

    You turn sharply and say, 'I'm sorry?'

    'Sorry …'

You raise your eyebrows and smile before sitting on the bench and taking out your phone. I sit down nearby and take out my phone too. After a while, you put yours away and look at me. I blush under your scrutiny, until at last you speak.

    'Got off at the wrong station as well?'

    'Well …'

You wait for me to elaborate, but I don't, so you rest your elbows on your knees and smile at me.

    'Is that a yes or a no?'

    'A … no.'

You look away, intrigued but wary.

We still have ten minutes to wait; you make
another attempt.

'So, what are you up to tonight?'

'Tonight?'

'You got any plans?'

I shake my head, but I love questions like this,
questions I can reuse: 'You got any plans?'

'I'm supposed to be meeting my mates at the next
stop. Got off too soon. They're waiting for me there
though, which is cool.'

'Cool.'

'Come out with us if you like.'

'If you like.'

Being on stage with you, my body seemed to listen
to yours, as though each move you made sent tiny
waves radiating towards me, through the air, to
pulse against me. It was too much and not enough,
all at once.

**

Early again, I waited outside the back door of the
theatre, at the top of the steel steps leading up the
eastern wall. I watched you come clanging up those
steps towards me, a dark chasm of a construction site

47

between you and the city lights, something building around us like the layers of a slow, sure song.

Inside the dark, windowless theatre, Lara retreated with her script to the back row, leaving the two of us alone in the dim light of the stage. We were so close to each other I could hear you breathing and smell the salt of your body, mingled with sweat and tobacco. It was so easy to be at your mercy.

In the woods, a sign reads: 'Sculptures in the Trees: An Exhibition'. We wander around, studying the structures, the way they play with light and sound. Your favourite is a giant twisting curve of reinforced glass; mine is a large concrete cylinder, on its side, like a stormwater drain.

I spread out a picnic blanket. You pour wine, feed me cheese, but you won't meet my gaze. I can hardly breathe, waiting for you to say something.

When you do, it's such a relief I almost don't hear the words:

'You know I don't love you.'

'Love you,' I whisper, touching your face.

'Though I like the way you touch me.'

I close my eyes and say, 'Touch me.'

And you do, but only to remove my hand from your cheek, saying, 'I wish you wouldn't do that.'

'Do that?'

'That. Repeat everything. It doesn't make for great conversation.'

I look up at you, smile a little and say, 'Conversation?'

Lara told us to go out together after that scene.

'You're still awkward around each other,' she said. 'The audience needs to believe you're lovers.'

So there we were in Hyde Park, traipsing across the grass, trouser hems soaking up the wet. There'd been a thunderstorm that evening and the sky was a dark wash of grey above white-barked trees, smooth-skinned benevolent creatures, watching. I looked up, I remember this, my eyes drawn by a pulse of lightning, far off to the west, probably over the sea. And my hand felt cold and stiff, clutching my beer in its brown paper bag.

The silence between us was spacious, like the night. Like you. The last bird had gone quiet; in its wake, a choir of insects had taken up the song, accompanied by a steady drub of frogs.

Near a low-walled fountain under one of the park's aged fig trees, we sat with our backs to the bulging mass of trunk. You used that penguin bottle opener you kept on your keyring and handed me my beer, wet with condensation and still icy cold. I took it, ran my hair behind my ear.

'Too awkward, hey?' I said.

'Apparently so.'

You smiled and I fidgeted with the grass, tore at it, needing something to do with my hand to stop it reaching for you, though I felt quite sure I'd be allowed to one day. That all the waiting was just a game, a ritual we had to enact to please the time gods, to maintain the illusion that time is linear, though everyone knows it's actually circular, looping this way and that, folding over on itself such that you and I were already lovers in some other dimension.

The grass was too wet beneath us so you stood up and held out your hand for me. It was warm and dry, the same hand I'd held in rehearsals, and yet not the same because this time it was spontaneous, unscripted.

'Come on,' you said, not letting go. I ran behind you, my bag thumping against my hip, the air fresh and damp on my cheeks like ocean spray.

**

Walking behind you along the open corridor to your door, two weeks into the season, I barely noticed the early moon or the swirling swallows, or the pot plants that supposedly beautified those ugly red brick walls. I was thinking about the way you kissed me on stage, so slowly, and how strange it was that an audience already so quiet could somehow go quieter still.

Your place was small, with all four rooms leading off a tiny entrance hall. There were two low sofas in the lounge room, and a guitar on a stand.

'Have a seat,' you said, opening French doors on to a tiny balcony overlooking the car park below. Life was loud outside, laughter from somewhere, sudden pulses of music. The branches of nearby trees brushed against the railings and you offered to make me some chamomile tea. I can still see your face as you delivered it to my hands in that funny old cup, green with leaf shapes carved into it. That easy smile.

'Narcissus's mother was a naiad, did you know that?' you said, picking up your guitar and sitting down with it. 'Called Liriope.'

Sounded like another language in your mouth.

'What's a naiad?'

'A water nymph. His father was a river god: Cephissus.'

I blew tiny ripples into my tea. 'So what does

that make Narcissus? A river god too? A water prince?'

'Something like that,' you said, a dimple creasing your cheek as you arranged your fingers on the neck and began to play.

'Sounds like someone else I know,' I said. I knew about your daily surf; you'd told me already that nothing short of a hailstorm could keep you from it. I closed my eyes to listen to your melody as it merged with the sounds of the city and the dusk-song of birds gathering on the tree outside your window.

You take hold of my hair, pull my head back so that my throat and jaw are bared, like prey, and I am frozen, hardly breathing lest you should stop. You run your face along my throat, first your cheek and then your lips, soft. Then you take my head in your hands and look into my eyes, saying, 'Who are you?'

'You,' I say, because that's all I have become: a reflection of you.

You release one hand to stroke my hair off my face. The breathing is loud between us. You lean in close, as though you might kiss me, but then you look away and stand back.

'This isn't going to work,' you say. 'I'm sorry.'

'I'm sorry?'
'I tried. I thought maybe I could … love you …'
'Love you.'
'I have to go.'
'Go?'

I can still see your face, caught in the stage lights as
you walked between the wire and plaster sculptures,
past that sculpture made from broken shards of mirror.
I can see the tenderness in your face as you smiled at
your fractured reflection and moved closer, though
I wasn't meant to be looking at you. I was meant to
be trailing my fingers along the damp wall of the
cylindrical sculpture, humming a tune, finishing the
water in the wine bottle. Lying down as an audio-track
of restful, slowing breathing began to play.

**

It was a Sunday evening, no show to turn up for,
but there you were anyway, leaning against the
doorframe, dark curls falling across your face.

'Hi,' you said, tucking them back over your ear.
I wanted to say come in, but the sight of you made
the words melt like gold flakes on my tongue.

'Do you want to get something to eat?' you said,
so easily, as if this was now the natural order of

things. Happiness coursed through me, a torrent of joy so potent it scared me for all the promise of loss it held.

We walked together beneath whispering trees. The night air was cool and the silk of my gold dress brushed against my skin. I kept catching you looking at it, your eyes drawn to its shimmer, its softness. You laughed at something I said and put your arm around me, and I knew it was coming.

'You're too much,' you said. 'I can't take it.'

'You can take it,' I said, managing to hold your gaze, emboldened by your tone, your arm around my shoulders. You stopped walking, held my hand to make me stop too.

It was so soft, that kiss—no trace of Narcissus's cruelty then, no lights, no audience holding its collective breath. It was only my breath in the darkness, and yours.

**

I see you, Narcissus, brought down by desire. Brutal, isn't it? The way it barrels through, trailing grief and longing behind it.

'Why?!' you shout at the reflection that won't let you close enough.

The image shouts too, same time, same word.
You put your hand to the glass, don't hear me in my
concrete cave, echoing,
'Why? Why?'
And you scoff at yourself: fool for your own face.
'There is no hope for me,' you murmur. 'I will never
know love.'
'No hope,' I whisper. 'No love.'

You sank to the floor as a second audio-track of breathing began, heavier than the first one, slightly out of synch. Both tracks slowed to silence as the lights dimmed and all was dark.

I found it eerie, every night, pretending to be dead, the unflinching stillness of it. The applause came as a relief, a kind of resuscitation.

**

I watched from the bed as you pushed a towel into your bag. I can barely think about this now, much less recount it, but I have started, and so I must finish, and maybe when everything is recorded, every last detail, you will emerge from the page, like a tapestry or one of those macramé creations, woven out of the golden threads of my memories.

You came to me, put your arms around me and

rested your forehead on mine, your lovely forehead with those very faint lines. I can still trace the shape of your hairline in the air in front of me. I'm doing it now.

'You're so sweet when you're sulking,' you said.

'I'm not sulking,' I said, though I was, of course. 'I just wish you'd let me come with you.'

'I'd love to have you there,' you said, jabbing me gently in the ribs, 'but you know I spend more time with you than I do with Anthony these days.'

I smiled but it wasn't your old friend I envied; it was the ocean itself, the way you looked at it, as if you couldn't breathe without it. The way you would leave me for it every morning, leave me to wake up alone and wanting your warmth beside me in bed instead of seeping out into that watery vastness.

'Okay,' I said, 'go on, be free.'

I offered to drop you off at the island ferry because that would give me more time with you, just a bit more time.

We arrived at the terminal and you got out, opening the boot, letting in a whoosh of sea air and the rocking, creaking, clanging sounds of the wharf. A cruise liner was docked nearby, gargantuan against the sky, a towering city all its own.

'Come on, brother,' you said to Anthony, 'let's get moving.'

You dropped the car keys into my outstretched palm.

'Have fun, boys,' I said, though what I meant was: *please don't go.*

'Not too much fun though, right?' you said, kissing me, shutting out everything but the surge and slap of water, the ting-ting-ting of steel on concrete. 'I'll miss you.'

'You will not,' I smiled.

Anthony was ahead, near the terminal already.

'Oh yes I will,' you said, hoisting your bag on to your shoulder and picking up your board. 'And you'd better miss me.'

I should have said: *I will … I always will.* I should have run after you, gone with you, no matter what you'd said. But I didn't because I wanted to be serene, self-contained, the antithesis of Echo, waiting for you but not too hard. And so I let you go, watched you smile and walk away, wind-whipped into the glare.

That was the last I saw of you, disappearing into brightness, into a light as ethereal as the one you'd emerged from on that first rehearsal afternoon. As though you were leaving by the same unearthly portal that had let you in.

**

The pines stand dark and moaning now against a heavy sky. Rain and white horses jag across the sea, cursing it, as I do, for taking you away. For letting Anthony be the one to ride the ferry home alone, lugging two surfboards instead of one and carrying your weekend bag, yours until you fell off your board and hit the reef.

Your beautiful head, lifeless.

Your blood, pluming into the water, taking the essence of you—of both of us—into the coldest, deepest, darkest of places. Into the depths of that ocean you always smelled of, that place you loved more than me. Not that you had a choice, I know. You were just an ocean creature, of the water not the land. No-one can tell me why, but out of the light you came to me, and back into it you went, going home, no more now than a shimmer on the darkening skin of the sea.

Small Disturbances

Yvonne Edgren

Liv sits in the sun, on the bottom step of the back verandah. She's been collecting snails for the blue-tongue that lives under there somewhere but now she watches as one of her captives slides over her bare foot with its waving eyes extended. Running as fast as it can, she thinks. The snail is cold and wet, but her foot and the sun are both warm so that the snotty trail it leaves behind dries straight away and shrinks, tightening on her skin. The whole effect is ticklish, and interesting. She hears the flyscreen door bang shut behind her, and turns to see her farmor, her grandmother, gazing at her.

'Ah, you're feeding your lizard again,' Ebba says, looking at the ice-cream container full of snails at Liv's side.

'Yes, Farmor, but not this one, she's my friend.' Liv prods at one of the wavering eyes which immediately withdraws back into the snail's head. Tiring of this, Liv moves her attention to her grandmother's working jaw.

'You haven't got your fangs, show me!'

Both the old woman and the little girl have gaps in their mouths, some of which match. Liv's gaps are common to everyone her age and are slowly filling with new teeth but Farmor's gaps are uniquely connected to her own history. Liv still hopes they might grow back. Farmor calls her false teeth her 'foreign fangs'. They live on her bedside table overnight, and she sometimes forgets to put them in, or chooses not to. Ebba obligingly opens her mouth wide, making the line that runs up from her jaw pucker a bit. Liv scrambles off the bottom step to make a closer inspection.

'Anything?' asks Ebba.

'No, still just gum. How about mine?'

Liv lifts her face and opens wide so her grandmother can get a good view of her teeth. Ebba peers in at the pinkly shining gums, seeing the gaps

61

between milk teeth where little pearly domes are breaking the surface of the flesh like newly emerging mushrooms. There is also some breakfast in there.

'Oh yes, they're growing very quickly! But if you want to keep them you'd better go and brush your teeth. You don't want to end up with foreign fangs like mine, that would be fatal!'

Liv looks reproachfully at her grandmother. She likes foreign fangs, they are so fascinating with their yellow, perfectly shaped teeth wired to a pink plastic palate in just exactly the positions where they are needed. Why must she break off the morning's investigations and conversation for something as dull as toothbrushing? She heads off to the bathroom, but not before picking the snail off her foot and dropping it in Farmor's apron pocket.

'You have to mind my snail for me. And don't let any of Bluey's dinner escape or I'll be *very* cross, and then I won't check your teeth for you any more. Or let you play with my lizard. Or even *look* at it,' she adds.

'Oh dear, such threats! You're being very strict with me this morning,' says Ebba. 'I'll watch your snails, and if you show me that you can look after your teeth then I might be able to share the chocolate I have hidden in my room.'

'With Hector too?'

'Of course, with Hector too.'

Liv avoids eye contact as she flounces past on her way to the bathroom.

**

Hector, younger than Liv and without her knack for language, can only speak English, so Ebba relies on Liv to interpret. He knows the Swedish word for 'chocolate' though, and comes barrelling around the side of the house when Ebba calls to him to come and share some. When Liv returns, Ebba breaks the chocolate into three roughly equal pieces. The children begin reaching for their slab even before she is done and in her eagerness Liv manages to snap a corner off her piece so that she has two uneven shards, one larger than the other. Hector begins stuttering in indignant outrage.

'What does he say, Liv?' asks Ebba, baffled.

'He says it's not fair because I have two pieces and he only got one. I tried to tell him mine is just the same only broken but he's such a stupid baby!'

Liv's voice is starting to get louder, and Hector's lip is trembling with the hurt and injustice of the situation. Ebba suddenly feels tired, even though it is still only morning. Grimly, she snatches Hector's piece of chocolate and breaks it in half.

'There you go,' she says, 'now you have the same as your sister. Tell him, Liv.'

Hector's scowl clears as he listens to Liv. He sits down next to Ebba, pushing his face into her shoulder while Liv sits down on Ebba's other side.

'What did you say to him?'

'I said now he has two chocolates and they're both big. Look, one of mine is only little.' Liv holds up the broken corner of her slab.

'You're a clever girl, Liv,' Ebba murmurs, as Liv pushes closer so that she, too, can rest her head on Ebba's shoulder and softly stroke the scar on her cheek. The three of them sit like that for a while, enjoying their chocolate shards in companionable silence, while the forgotten snails in the ice-cream container make a slow break for freedom.

**

Ebba hears a series of chimes, like a clock but irregular. She peers out the window. As usual the sun is shining high in the wrong part of the sky. It is all indecipherable, the seasons as well as the hours, and she has felt herself held in suspension ever since she arrived in this temporally incoherent country to visit her son and his family. Time, for her, is a singularly Finnish phenomenon, measured in the festival songs of her minority language, in the growth and colour of things, their taste. Time is consumed. It is manifested and then devoured in the form of food appropriate to the season. Boiled young peas are eaten with melted butter and salt, while the Midsummer bonfire showers pagan sparks into the twilight and the fluorescent sun circumnavigates the sky, skimming the horizon like a skipped stone at its lowest, south-western point. In winter the sun struggles to heft itself to the treeline by lunchtime, which, if this is Thursday, consists of pea soup green as a fen. Here, time is dismembered, and now this absurd mis-chime reminds Ebba of how it has been left to flail.

'What are you doing, Farmor? Are you playing patience?' Liv interrupts Ebba's thoughts, leaning on the door frame, knowing not to enter Ebba's room without an invitation.

'I'm listening to the clock, can you hear it?' Ebba replies.

Liv looks puzzled and pokes her finger into her nose thoughtfully.

'Use your hanky, darling,' chides Ebba.

Liv tries to locate her pocket but the skirt she

is wearing has twisted sideways and the pocket is under her belly button where she can't find it. She stops her fumbling when the irregular chimes begin again. Without waiting for the invitation, she pushes past Ebba to get to the window.

'That's a rosella, Farmor! Did you think it was a clock?' She laughs, a bit derisively, Ebba thinks. How does the child know so much? This unkempt luck-child and her affinity with all the creatures crawling and perching in the garden, her endlessly poking fingers and peering eyes, her happy, easy fluency and ability to ask prying questions in two languages! Afraid of nothing, where has she come from? Ebba raises her hand to stroke the tousled head looking out the window but is brushed aside.

'Wouldn't you like me to replait your hair?'

Ebba imagines fondling Liv's long hair, yellow as wheat, while the child sits placidly accepting her ministrations.

'You can read to me instead. The one where she hangs their enemies up in a tree. I'll get the book.'

Liv reaches into the bookcase to retrieve the volume and then pulls the cane chair next to the bed, where she flops in happy anticipation.

'Here's your chair, you better find your glasses.'

It's a ritual. Ebba pretends not to know her

glasses are hanging around her neck. Liv allows
her to search for a while and then the glasses
are discovered in a moment of shared hilarity.
Recognising the ritual, Hector has sidled up to the
door and is watching them. Ebba waves him in,
reaching over the bed to grab a cushion and drop it
on the floor beside her.

'Tell him his picture book is on the dresser, Liv.'

Hector curls up on his nest at Ebba's feet. While
Ebba reads one book aloud in Swedish, Hector rifles
through the pages of the other book, interrupting
her occasionally with questions or observations that
Liv translates for him.

'He likes the picture where they've been sucked
up into the vacuum cleaner.'

'Yes,' responds Ebba, 'he always looks at that
one for a long time.'

She smiles down at him, and he grins back at
her. He loves this book but doesn't ever ask to take
it to his own room. She places her hand on his head,
knowing it won't be brushed away.

'Is it time we had something to eat?'

Liv leaps to the window,

'Let's ask the rosella!' she shouts, full of glee at
her own wit.

Ebba feels ashamed of herself. There is no derision in the child, there is only delight— delight with herself, with the world and with the moment. She gazes at Liv caught there on the bed in an amber shaft of sunlight, revelling in her untrammelled childhood and in the absurdity of meals determined by bird-time.

**

The constant traffic along the highway at the front of the house sounds as a rumble of white noise. It could just as easily be a waterfall or the wind soughing through trees, except for the occasional clang of a truck's metal doors, or the shriek and sigh of hydraulic brakes.

'Battle sounds,' thinks Hector.

He is watching Liv play with their matryoshka dolls. She has unpacked all nine layers and has them lined up on the circular dining table, like the spoke of a wheel, with the largest on the outside and the little peanut-sized one at the centre of the table. There was once a tenth, an even tinier baby that fitted inside the peanut but it was lost long ago. Liv is leaning down, with one eye closed, peering along the line of dolls as if sighting a rifle.

'They are all the same size,' she announces.

'They only look little because they're further away. The grandmother is the furthest!'

She is pleased with this conceit. It confuses the idea of nesting generations, who it is that holds whom, throwing open the question of which position she herself might occupy. Hector doesn't understand what she is talking about though, and stands impatiently waiting for her to shoot the dolls, wondering how far they will scatter.

**

Standing in the doorway of Ebba's room, just to look, Liv can see motes of dust flickering and sparkling in the golden light from the window.

'Look there,' she points, to show Hector. 'You can see the air!'

The children pass their arms rapidly through the beam of light, causing the dust to eddy and swirl. Part of the game is to flap arms without stepping over the threshold and entering the forbidden room. There are things here that are old and fragile, and not to be played with. The children stop their jostling to look. The room is full of objects that predate them, relics of lives their grandmother had before this one. The cane chair has a long tapestry draped over it that their grandmother has made herself, embroidering with wool made from dog hair that she has spun and dyed. It is faded, because the colours are made from onion skins, beetroot, rusty nails and other witchy ingredients that can't survive in bright foreign sunshine or modern times. The now muted browns, yellows and mauves are blended in a stylised design of flowers and coiling leaves on a striped ground. When she is allowed, Liv likes to trace the pattern with her finger, feeling the coarse hair so much rougher than wool, while Hector is curious about the dog but unsure how to frame his questions.

On the shelf above the bed, sits a one-eyed teddy bear, its fur worn off. He's an old gentleman teddy, in a three-piece suit and tie. He has some elastic braces to hold his pants up but they have perished and aren't able to support even themselves let alone a pair of trousers. Farmor has made the suit out of a real gaberdine one, cut up, and the shirt from a real dress shirt. Farfar's suit was worn out, beyond repair so she made clothes for the teddy so as not to waste the remaining fabric. It's one of two things they know about their farfar: he had a worn-out suit; and twice he went away to be a soldier, first as a boy and then again when he was a grown man. The teddy is very old and mustn't be played with because he is fragile. Liv knows he was played with a lot at one time, because of the worn fur and the eye, and because Farmor bothered to make a suit for him so he could be a gentleman rather than just a naked bear.

Another favourite thing is the bookcase. Sometimes the children are allowed to sit on the floor and look through the books. They are mostly very old, some have missing pages, or have lost their covers. There are picture books about mushroom families and flower people living in mossy forests full of fir trees. Some of the pictures are scary, lichen-covered boulders turn into trolls, or little gnomes with glowing eyes and red hats creep around farm houses on snowy nights while the occupants are asleep. There are also books with fewer pictures and more text, that tell strange, unsettling and sometimes wonderful stories that Farmor reads aloud. There is one about toys who are alive like real children, and have to be evacuated to Sweden by plane because they are too hungry. The one who is made of cloth and stuffed with toilet paper is so light that she is blown out of the plane by a puff of wind and is lost. For Liv, the toilet paper is the compelling detail in this narrative.

On Farmor's dressing table are some toy

soldiers, arranged in a line. They have round helmets
and are wearing white. Two soldiers are operating
a machine gun, one doing the shooting while the
other one supports a string of bullets. A third soldier
is lying on his stomach in the snow aiming his rifle
at an unseen enemy. The cold must be seeping into
his torso, stretched out as he is over the frozen
ground. The fourth and last soldier is on one knee,
with his rifle dangling by his side. He is looking
behind him and gesturing with his other arm as if to
say, 'Come on!'

But there is no-one there. Perhaps he has
friends, a blue-tongue with glowing eyes creeping
around under the farm house steps, or trolls hiding
behind mossy fir trees in the forest. Farfar will
come, with his gun, and blast the enemy into shards
of bone and shattered teeth, leaving their blood
steaming like hot breath in the snow. The children
are not allowed to touch the soldiers at all because
they are made of lead and are poisonous. If one were
to go in a mouth it could be fatal, Farmor has told
them. Even Hector is old enough not to go around
sucking things but Liv is afraid she would not be
able to resist putting the poison toy in her mouth,
just for the terror of it.

Through a Latte Darkly

John Jenkins

It's Wednesday morning, and I'm on my hands and knees outside Marco's glass doors, looking at a mat of tiny soap bubbles, a thin scumble of suds winking at me as they dry. He must have cleaned up the doorstep just a few minutes earlier, before opening.

There is no-one else around, luckily. My left elbow is stinging, from where I'd slipped and hit the cement, re-opening a wound from the night before. I pick myself up, balancing unsteadily; everything sparkles too brightly this morning, hurting my eyes.

Not a good start, and I still needed coffee. But

I won't tell Marco about my fall, because a normally alert person—one without a hangover, that is—would have stepped through easily. This morning, even with gumboots on, I would have slipped.

'And what would sir like—' Marco asks, as I stumble across him, '—besides a good kick in the pants?'

To most customers, he is a model of toothpaste-smile politeness.

'A café latte,' I say, and almost collapse on the counter.

**

I first met him at AA meetings. We were brothers in a way. It was a serious relationship, though on the surface seemed mostly fun and banter, as if the slightest hint of solemnity might kill the rapport.

This morning, Marco is firing up the coffee addict's favourite steam machine—then briskly levering the chrome handle down.

Smiling as ever, with his customary aplomb, he is immaculately dressed in pressed trousers, white shirt, a bow tie. Just the glance of a smile from him, as I look up. He immediately sees the cuts on my face—from an altercation the night before, or was it the night after that?

A hiss of steam, a sigh under his breath, then rich coffee flows.

With great gentleness, he reaches across now, running a careful finger along the worst scrape on my jaw. 'You know, my friend, you should really do "Shaving 101 and Basic Life Skills".'

I laugh nervously, and sip my latte. 'Thanks, pal.'

It's always good to be with Marco.

**

Six days later, and I'm feeling much better, my head almost clear, back at Marco's for my regular infusion. Though it's early, the place is full, and he moves with speed. I linger at my spot at the counter, sipping away, until people rush off to work and things go quiet.

'Do you remember when we first met?' he says. 'Back at the meetings? You know, it's more than five years now!'

As we talk, I show him some DVDs I'd just bought.

'Hitchcock, heh?' He glances at their covers, at *The Birds* and *Vertigo*, and considers. 'You know,' he says, 'I once did some acting. It was nothing much really, mostly on stage, then small parts on TV.'

He looks again at the cover artwork. 'As for

killer seagulls going psycho, I think you're safe
here. No birds in the café, that I can see. Not even
a sparrow.'

And smiles suddenly, 'You know, I can't resist a
cameo appearance.' He launches into an impromptu
impersonation of Alfred Hitchcock, enigmatically
poker-faced and sticking out his belly, pretending to
be double his weight.

I laugh, and sip my latte.

'Hey—this coffee is actually *good*!'

Marco feigns hurt. 'What did you expect! *My*
coffee is *the best*! As the *I Ching* says, perspiration
furthers!'

'That's persistence,' I correct him.

We talk a little about acting; then Marco recalls
the time he was an ambulance driver, then psych
nurse, before the major and almost terminal disaster
of his life, his failed pub business, followed by
alcoholism.

'When I tried to run that pub, I became my own
best customer! Nearly drank the place dry. What a
binge; always fabulously wasted.'

He brightens again. 'Now! Dah-dah! I have a
very special announcement for you!' And allows the
pause to linger, drawing it out.

'What?' I ask.

'I am going to … buy this café!'

'Bravo! Congratulations!' I pat him on the back, then glance at my watch. 'Hey—must go!'

'Any plans for tonight?'

'Yep, I'm um, er, going out.' I take a last sip, nod at my cup, then slyly change the subject, by complimenting him again. 'Another of your caffeine masterpieces.'

I had half expected some sort of lecture. But that's not Marco's style. Instead, he pirouettes on his impossibly shiny shoes, grabs a checked cloth, and deftly swipes everything in sight. 'Enjoy … Enjoy!' he says. 'But not too much …'

**

It's Friday early, 'the day after' again … or one after that, or … I've lost all track of things. Now find myself tottering on a vertiginous café stool, with my eyes half shut, head in hands.

Marco considers the vision of barely functioning humanity before him, then with a careful and concerned scrutiny. 'You remember,' he begins, 'how I once drove ambulances? It was years before the pub episode, when I still had my wits intact?'

I nod, waiting.

'It was great to feel useful,' he says. 'Ambulance

driving was good, but I certainly don't miss
the stress!'

'Right,' I grunt.

'Look!' he says, 'Now! I want to wake you up!
It's my way of administering a bit of CPR.' And
with great care, he takes a small coin-like medallion
from his wallet. Its shining inscription cuts right
through my early-morning haze. It says *Five
Years, Recovering.*

Impressed and suddenly sober, I see Marco in
a much more vulnerable light, as he carefully puts
the precious object back into his wallet; his hands
now trembling; eyes brimming with tears of pride
and sadness.

I feel overwhelmed, and am about to say things
he does not wish to hear, perhaps some sort of lame
excuse about my own situation, when he shakes his
head, abruptly flicking a cloth over one shoulder.

'Don't say anything! No need to. Neither of us
can stand sanctimonious penny lectures, or finger
wagging! I just want to see you better. And get
clean again.'

He stands there, very sombre, now slightly
shaking his head.

'Life is just one big light bulb joke,' I say.

'That's right, my friend.'

He stares at me, I feel embarrassed but he continues. 'You know the pledge I made. *I am responsible when anyone reaches out for help.* The pledges we both made, remember ... And all the rest of it.'

He pours a coffee, and places it on the counter.

I groan darkly as Marco, watching my train-wreck of an expression, pushes the cup very slowly across the counter with his little finger.

'Now, here's an exercise for you, to start the day nicely. So let's imagine that's a drink, a real drink. Oh yeah, it's not even a "serious" drug, you protest, not a real addiction. It's just common old alcohol. Hey—and everyone drinks. Of course you want it. You have hundreds of excuses. Yes, I know them all. But, look, *I'm not giving it to you.*' He smiles, as the cup just sits there, reflected in the polished wood, dumbly obeying gravity.

'It's not going anywhere, is it?'

Then I look up. 'This is getting bizarre, Marco.'

'So what do you want to do, my friend? What's your strategy now, how do you deal with it? You don't have to feel ashamed. Come back to the meetings, please, that might be a start. *Fall over, and ...*'

'Yeah, I know ... *get back up again.*' I stare in

silence. Wondering, can I really do it?

'Boo!' he shouts, and I nearly have a heart attack.

'Now get out of here, and go home.' Crossing his arms. 'And don't come back, my friend, unless you've done some serious talking to that light bulb, the one still hanging dead and neglected from the ceiling in your own private little rat-hole.'

**

It's a bright autumn morning, two months later; two grinding, strung-out months later. But I have made the effort, as I explained to him on the phone. And I've finally written the first three chapters of my new book, on my favourite film directors. I've been talking about it for almost a year. Just talk, until now. And Marco wants me to celebrate.

Not a hint of suds outside, just freshness and birdsong. And I'm clean-shaven, in a new suit, and feeling happy.

As I walk in, a brand new sign above the café says, *Marco's*.

Marco is beaming when I walk to the counter. I congratulate him on his café, and new sign. He considers, thoughtfully, 'The journey of a thousand leagues ...'

I complete the saying for him: '... begins with

a dive into a pool of suds and a bloody elbow … At least, for me.'

'So what would sir like?' he sparkles.

He's in one of his very best moods, I see.

'My usual café latte, please Marco.'

'Is that small, regular, large?' He is barely holding it in, indulging himself with a friendly laugh at my expense, which is also his way of celebrating that I'm back on track.

It feels like old times, after we'd first met at AA meetings and soon became friends. After so many downers, it was great to fool around and joke with Marco, all the while seriously going out of our way to help each other. Then he got truly clean and I, well, slipped a little, and then a lot.

I make a glass-to-lip gesture.

But he keeps on … 'Does sir have a "keep cup" for the environmentally conscious? Or would you like your coffee in a corrugated or styrofoam receptacle?'

I catch on, and encourage his impromptu comedy routine, feeding him the next line …

'In a mug, or a cup?' he persists. 'Or would sir prefer a tumbler, wine glass, flute, shot, stem, lute, bassoon, oboe?' he demands. 'Would you like Fair Trade coffee, or a big fat exploiter? Or perhaps some smooth, hand-crafted, doubly caffeinated bliss for the discerning connoisseur?'

I open my mouth, just about to answer, but nothing can stop him now.

'Full-bodied, triple-roasted or smooth? Costa Rica, La Cascada? How about Arabica Robusta?'

Every now and then he bangs his flashy parfait spoon down with a loud clunk on the counter, just for emphasis.

'Don't forget, we also have vanilla, mocha and beta blocker?'

There's a tiny pause in his rapid patter, but I'm not quite quick enough to jump in.

'A cappuccino,' he continues, 'or chai-latte? A babycino, perhaps? Or would you prefer a skinny-thingo?'

He slows right down now. 'Does sir really understand *delayed gratification*? Can sir cultivate enough willpower, cleverness, strategy—whatever it takes—for you to understand that?'

'Well, just look at me,' I say, posing in my new suit. 'The longer I wait, then the better ...'

'... it gets.' He completes the old AA wisdom. Then Marco changes tack, gesturing at framed photos of coffee cups behind him, smiling enigmatically.

'You see, sir, I am also a creative artist! Deftly, I sculpt highly decorative designs, in the froth of your glass—from a great variety of floral or abstract motifs. And today, just for you, I will lovingly render a miniature galactic corkscrew, inscribed in hot, swirling froth—a reference to Hitchcock's *Vertigo*.' Marco makes me a wonderful latte, complete with charming spiral.

'Mind if I join you, mate?' he says, suddenly dropping the act. 'It's my first for the day.'

We sit down together at an empty table near the window, and life seems more benign here, as we watch the morning sun outside.

'Cheers, my friend,' he says suddenly, and we clink cups, the sweet coffee steam rising.

We both know it won't be easy. We've been through all this before. But, this time, I'm feeling strangely optimistic.

'Two months,' I say. 'Two whole months.'

A Single Life

Marian Matta

At 7:12 am the night shift nurse distilled Nell's recent history into a series of dot points.

'Bed 8, Mrs Eleanor Radcliff, seventy-eight years old, brought to Emergency yesterday with compound fractures of the left radius and ulna, severe laceration to left forearm, and hypovolemic shock.' She peered over her glasses and briefly dropped the brisk tone. 'Fell off a stepladder hanging curtains, caught a glass vase on the way down. Lucky to be alive.

'Right,'—she was all business again—'brought up to the ward late last night after surgery, plates and screws in the breaks, one unit of blood beforehand, on her third unit now, blood obs every fifteen on the quarter hour, BP eighty over fifty but finally rising. Uncommunicative. She seems agitated.'

At morning teatime, as Nell refused the offer of a cup of tea, Margo the social worker found Phillip Radcliff's number on her phone.

'Phillip. He's a relative? Next of kin? I'll ring Phillip, shall I?'

Nell shook her head, maintained her fixed gaze out of the window for a few seconds more. Then, crumpling into her pillows as if all resolve had failed, said, 'All right. If you must. But I don't want to talk to him. Just let him know I'm okay, no need to worry, no need to come. Is that cup of tea still on offer?'

By eight that evening a couple of the staff were finding excuses to pass by Bed 8 and catch a glimpse of the man who sat there, holding Nell's hand as she slept.

'I thought Margo said her husband was coming.'
'She did.'
'But he wouldn't even be fifty.'
'And a bloody good fifty at that.'
'Mid, late forties, I'd say, absolute tops.'
'She must be rich. Or she's got hidden charms.'
'Bitch.'

**

Nell's eyes fluttered open. Phillip had the distinct impression she'd been awake a while. He leaned in to stroke her hair and brush his lips against hers, just below the oxygen cannula.

'Welcome back, sweetheart. Good sleep?'

'Hello, darling. So you came anyway.'

'Of course I came. You knew I would. Got a direct flight from Brisbane.'

'And the conference?'

'Fuck it.'

His thumb soothed the back of her hand where a fine tube disappeared into bluing skin.

'I spoke to the doctor. She says once this crazy blood pressure settles down you're out of here.'

'It's settling as we speak. As *you* speak.'

They rode the next wave of silence together, eyes locked, thoughts engaged, but when he spoke, Phillip's voice was sharper, louder, causing the nurses' ears to prick up.

'Damnit, Nell, why the curtains? I told you I'd do them soon as I got back home.'

'But I don't want to be reliant on you for everything. I keep trying to tell you, I don't want to be helpless, dependent. You don't know what it's like …'

He sighed, rested his head on her thin thigh.
'I love you, Nell Radcliff, you exasperating,
wonderful woman.'

Waves encircled their ankles, drained sand through
their toes. Their rock seat was smooth and sun-
warmed. Nell leaned into Phillip, cleared her throat,
and launched into what she had to say.

'I've been thinking. Since the fall, I've been
thinking of so many things. Or maybe they're just
the one thing over and over. I've been thinking
about people's lives, the way we get a single shot at
it, and something goes wrong or we get the rough
end of the stick, then that's it, and it doesn't matter
if ninety-nine people have great lives because that
last life, that one which fails, that life belongs to
someone and it's the only one they get and they have
to live it, and it doesn't matter to them that they're
in a tiny minority because it's a hundred per cent of
their life which is fucked up.'

She paused to draw breath but Phillip held his
silence, knowing this was just an introduction.

'And even if we start with a clear run, good
health, good prospects, we can bring it all to ruin by
making a bad choice—'

'Like hanging curtains on your own?'

'—or worse, we can bring someone else's life to ruin. We get to make real choices if we're lucky enough, and I made my big one right here on this beach thirty years ago. I chose you. But did you get a real choice? Or did I simply overwhelm you with mine?'

'Thanks for making me sound like a five-year—'

'Look at this.' She raised her arm, the great gash of a scar still flaring across her wrist, the neater surgical scar below it, but it was the skin, crêpey and alien, which she brushed with her fingers. 'I'm getting ancient, Phillip, skin like old cinema curtains—way before your time, see, even my cultural references are from the Stone Age—and even if I stay healthy to the end I'll still be a burden to you, and what will you get in return for your loving attention?'

'Nell, don't—'

'Don't worry. Whatever happens, I'll exit dancing. It's just that you've spent your whole life with someone who was already on the downhill slide—'

'Hardly.'

'—and you never got the good years, the years when I was always strong and in control and, you know, *fresh*.'

Phillip couldn't hold back the laugh which came bubbling up. 'Fresh? Darling, you were warm and sweet and fresh as a peach. And you still are. And you always will be in my eyes.'

'But what if I get some hideous disease, what if I get cancer or lose my marbles? You could have years shackled to a living corpse. How can I ask someone as young as you to risk a future like that?'

'I don't want to talk about such things. It's nothing to bother us for a long, long time. Maybe never. Anyway, we've been through all this before and my answer's always the same—this is the life I chose, the life with you. How many lives does one man need?'

'Oh, those conversations! They were all hypothetical, *what if?* rather than *what now?* But I want you to think about it again. All of it. I want you to picture yourself with someone your own age. Or younger, damnit! Imagine your life with someone who can give you all the stuff you missed out on by being with me. Maybe even that kid we never quite had. Will you promise to do that?'

'I promise. If that's what it'll take to calm you again. But you know what my conclusion will be: *Love is not love which alters when it alteration finds.*'

'Piffle. Pretty, romantic words, but I want you

to test it. Check out those luscious creatures up the beach there, flaunting their wares, all firm flesh and moist invitations.'

She nodded at a group of teenage girls cavorting self-consciously in the shallow surf below the lighthouse. Phillip glanced their way then hugged Nell close and gave her a mock stern look.

'Ah, now I see what this is all about. You've met a new fellow, haven't you. Was it in hospital? Some medical lothario? Sad-eyed patient? Minx. I can't let you out of my sight.'

'You've sprung me, darling.' She laughed but the laughter didn't light up her eyes. 'I had a life before you came along, a good, full, exciting life. But I'm a tough old bird, and by the time I fall off the twig I'll have eaten up all of your good life.'

'It's just the accident making you talk like this.'

'I know, love, I know.'

A seagull seemed to catch Nell's attention as it swooped above the waves, and Phillip hoped the uncomfortable conversation had worked itself out, but then she delivered her conclusion.

'I don't want you just to think about it. I want you to, well, to get out there and see how it feels again.'

'No!'

'Not even to humour me?'

'No.'

They both heard the paper-thin edge of uncertainty.

He sent a text about going up to the big smoke for the evening, late business arrangement, some rubbish that they both knew was a lie, and he hated himself with every finger tap on the phone screen. At the highway out of Geelong, where the sign pointed home along the Great Ocean Road, it took a huge effort of will to flick on the right indicator and turn north. An hour later he was in the bathroom of their tiny flat in Melbourne, showered and shaved and ready for what the evening might bring.

He stood a long time in front of his reflection, casting a coldly critical eye over the man who stared back at him. Forty-eight—the same age Nell had been when they met. *If I step out of this marriage right now I could still have a fabulous, rewarding life, just like Nell's life with me. This doesn't have to be the brink of a lonely old age. Okay, Nell, those girls on the beach. You know what I really think? They make me wonder how the hell you could have been attracted to me when I was that stupidly immature. Oh yes, and there's one other thought: when I picture me with one of them it feels—no, I'd never say this to your face—kind of obscene. I begin to see how bloody brave you were to take me seriously.*

And he was recalling the disapproving stares, the thirty years of skyward glances when he and Nell kissed in public. They'd both overheard the remarks: *Yuk! That's gross! I thought she was his mother.*

He sucked in his lean gut, flexed his muscles, examined his fine features. Not bad, all of it not bad, no shopping mall slouch, no beer gut Homer Simpson. He could still turn heads of a more approving kind. But how long would Nell live? Healthy and strong despite her fears, she had another fifteen years left in her, easy. A widower at sixty-five; was that too late to chart a different course and begin again? Better to do it now while the lingering charms of boyhood clung to him, while 'middle-aged' was still a term which sat uncomfortably on his broad shoulders, and 'elderly' was beyond imagining.

And yet, about to head into the seething world of desperate singles, wasn't he just looking like a sad old bastard trying to pull a younger chick? *Doing this for you, Nell*, he thought. The gallows humour brought a grimacing smile to his mouth.

Discreet Net searching had thrown up a

place off King Street that sounded okay, not too frightening for a reminted virgin nightclubber. He spent an hour or so at the bar, checking out the scene, seeing how it was done these days, then, just as he considered ending the charade and making an early exit, a hand was laid on his arm and a sweet voice pitched high against the music said, 'Come and dance with me.'

The woman who led him onto the dancefloor had maybe a decade over the nubile beach nymphs yet to Phillip she still seemed impossibly young. Whatever feats of engineering kept her lowcut dress in place as she danced in a sinuous, confident manner, it was clear that the breasts beneath were high and firm and in no need of scaffolding. *Not like Nell's.* His wife's breasts, still generous and full, now victims of time, of gravity, and their own ripeness; where the soft flesh fell away, Nell's chest revealed dips and hollows which he couldn't have imagined when they first made love in that glorious, transgressive euphoria.

'Penny for them.'

'What? Oh …' Phillip's face flushed, he shrugged. 'Breasts. I was thinking about breasts. That sounds awful.'

But she laughed, throwing her head back

and offering up the pale stretch of her throat, the firmness below.

'I *thought* you were giving the girls a close look. Hey, it's okay, don't be embarrassed.'

When she winked at him, raised her arms high and executed a quick twirl for his delight, Phillip wasn't alone in his admiration.

At the flat, Phillip's first action was to close all the blinds, as if the lights of Melbourne, stretching down to the dark bay, were all eyes watching and judging.

The girl looked around. 'You live here?'

'No. It's just a bolthole for when we're—I'm in town.'

'From where?' It was just conversation, no real interest behind it.

'Hobart.'

The lie slipped out easily. Only Bass Strait between it and the truth.

'And what do you do down there?'

'I'm an architect.'

She nodded approval. 'So you'd have a nice modern home yourself, I guess.'

No, he wanted to say, *we live in a small house by the beach. It's old and comfortable and has no airs and graces, but it was my wife's home and we've never wanted anything more because it's filled with the best memories. And you, young lady, I hope you have such memories when you're my age.*

'No, it's old but I love it.'

'So.' She inclined her head to his left hand, 'Divorced? Stepping out for a while? The white ring mark,' she explained in answer to his puzzled look. 'Such a giveaway. Plus you seem a little ... out of practice, shall we say. Not that it matters. None of my business.'

He didn't know how to answer.

When she slipped off her jacket her skin was smooth and beautiful, her arms firm. Philip began unbuttoning his shirt, watching as she eased her shoulder straps down. Something stirred in his guts, but it wasn't lust.

'I'm sorry.' He buttoned up his shirt again. 'It's all a mistake. Here, let me call you a taxi. I'll pay. I'm really sorry.'

Ninety minutes later he was re-entering Aireys Inlet, and his heart surged as it always did when the Split Point light came into view; it meant home, it meant happiness, it meant Nell. She'd be asleep by now. Or maybe lying awake, wondering what was going on. Either way, their bed didn't feel like the right place for him to be at that moment. He passed the end of their street and headed up to the lighthouse, blinking a warning into the night. Its comforting rhythm, usually a source of reassurance, felt more like an accusation on this clear night. He parked at the tower's base and stared out across the ocean, let the dark waves lull him back into a state of calm.

Ridiculous. You're such a fool, Phillip.

The ocean's growling voice carried him back to that first night under the light, himself barely out of school, Nell already on the cusp of another stage. She'd been beautiful, vibrant, radiating life and freedom and forbidden temptations. She'd passed him the joint, watched him with sleepy-eyed curiosity as he sucked in the smoke. *Are you a friend of Tom's?* And he'd flushed and stumbled, told her he was holidaying with his parents, had just wandered down to what sounded like a good beach party. *Parents*, she'd repeated, but her little laugh hadn't been at his expense. *So much life ahead of you. So many paths to follow. I'm Nell, by the way.* And, *Phillip*, he'd replied as he clasped her outstretched hand and felt for the first time that heat and desire which had burned through the years and warmed him still, even as his skin puckered under the cool moonlight.

And it hadn't ever just been about the sex, not even at the start. She'd been—he grinned at the memory—an *education*. Like a living encyclopaedia she'd brought a world of ideas to him then examined his responses, crammed her forty-eight years of knowledge into his raw and hungry eighteen, and left him craving more. *You'd have been a great mother. I might even have been a passable dad with your help. Hell, if that kid we started had made it, I might've been a grandfather by now.* But that last-gasp menopausal pregnancy had bled away into lost promise, and he'd been too young back then to yearn for what had gone, yet he'd sensed Nell's wistfulness under her wry-smiled dismissal. No fatherhood for him now, not if he stayed.

'Ah, they'd just put me in a nursing home,' he said to the night. *And I'll never do that to you, Nell, never.*

The first flush of sunrise was already spilling over the horizon by the time he turned the car into their driveway. Held in its glow, the familiar world reasserted itself. He eased into their bed, curled around Nell's thin frame, felt the familiar rush of pleasure as she snuggled into the comforting crescent of his body.

'Cold,' she murmured, pulling his arm around her.

'Not on the inside.'

'Good night?'

'Yes. No. Yes. Tell you about it over breakfast.'

Her breathing settled back into the rise and fall of bony ribs. She was calm, the all-knowing woman who held his life in the circle of her hands. A Saturday morning sunbeam sneaked through a gap in the curtains and edged across her body. If Phillip squinted his eyes, her shape against the light was the same sensuous curve he'd seen the night he fell in love with her, when hormone-driven teenage lust transformed into a stunning realisation that, ridiculous as it seemed, the universe had chosen to present him with The One. And nothing had really changed since then; bodies, fashion—what did any of it mean? It was all just window dressing.

Suffused with certainty, he nuzzled into the nape of her neck, inhaled her sweet and earthy scent with its lifetime of memories. Nell's soft grey curls tickled his nose as he matched his breathing to hers, and soon enough he was wrapped in a deep, untroubled sleep.

London via Paris and Rome

Andreas Å Andersson

We moved to a new share house on Union Street and from there on it was all home brew, new faces and an evening sun setting fire to a backyard brick wall. Mitch was supposedly Mum's second cousin and emptied the storage room facing the laneway when he got her call. At the time, we didn't need much space and except for the torn carpeting and a damp smell there was nothing wrong with the place. Ron called it a dunghole, but if anything, it had a late '60s working class charm. It was my first summer in Melbourne since coming down from Horsham so I didn't know what to expect. It was also my only summer. Sometime in April we were leaving for London, indefinitely, making stops in Paris and Rome.

I was waiting for a call from the council that didn't come and Ron had finally gotten into construction which meant good money but early mornings—not once did I hear him leave for work. Downstairs was Myra. She had a military crew cut and didn't say much, but was always there, sipping peppermint tea or taking notes in her My Little Pony journal. Tony had the room next to ours and was the proud owner of the household's 3-in-1 rice cooker.

'Look at this coating,' he said, one hand digging in on the grains, the other spinning a strainer between us. 'All starch. It all comes down to rinsing. One go is not enough. How could it be?'

I smiled, thinking it was especially funny since his hair didn't look like it'd been shampooed all year. He wanted to show me a lot of things, Tony. I found it cute. Every day at noon he made us fried rice for breakfast. Usually just with green peas but every once in a while with chicken or egg, whatever he could find. He had a lazy eye that he tried to cover with his long fringe. I pretended not to notice it. That first day, while fiddling with the stereo, Tony asked if I liked Spoon, and thinking it was a drug I said yes. Even Myra laughed.

**

We'd ditched Ron's bed base and just kept the
twin-sized mattress. It was his idea to start scaling
down on possessions before the big move. With
the addition of a couple of picnic quilts it was as
comfortable as ever. Alone in our room, Ron rattled
on about the Eiffel Tower, the Colosseum, Big Ben.
I sat behind him, stabbing my knuckles in his upper
back. His long shifts made him sore all the way
down the sides. With my eyes I followed the twigs
in the saffron-coloured wallpaper. Like the pattern
coiled, so did his thoughts.

'Do you know how many steps there are to the
top? Five hundred? More than that. It's seven. Think
of that.'

I thought of that and I leaned in to get more
pressure.

'Do you think I should cut my hair?' I said. He
didn't reply. Then he said: 'Imagine us at the top.
You have to take the elevator the last bit but then
you step out on this tiny platform and it's all right
there. The sky, the city. The wind violent, I'm sure.
Hair covering our faces. Such a great shot. We'll
frame it and hang it over our headboard.'

It wasn't a bad picture. Something out of a film.
I reckoned I'd do okay in it.

When it was time for Ron to crash I closed the door and went down to the others. Ron said my sighs kept him awake and I didn't want to be that person.

Mitch worked irregular hours and sometimes hung out with us in the somewhat shady backyard, slumped in one of the couches. Tony was sucking on an unlit cigarette, his naked feet in a ray of sunlight that sneaked in through the neighbours' plum trees. No-one in the house cared enough to water the plants, except the one cannabis plant appropriately flowering in a reused bucket of fertilisers. Still, English ivy was flourishing and covering most of the northern fence.

'When are you off?' Mitch said. 'Not that I mind having you here.'

'You should ask Ron. He would know.'

'Booked your flight?'

'Don't think so.'

'Maybe it's too early.'

Tony straightened his legs to keep the sunbeam in reach. 'Where were you going again?' he said, the cigarette now hidden in his closed fist. His elbow was resting on an empty flower pot, an arm frozen in a throwing motion. It was an odd image. It looked like he was holding a hand grenade, directing it towards me. I stared at it and his one straight eye and forgot what he had asked.

'I haven't seen much of Ron,' Mitch said. 'What's he like?'

'Oh he's great.'

'The good ol' *great* guy,' he said. 'What makes him great?'

'A lot. Trevor Larkins's his uncle.'

Mitch didn't get it.

'He was a half-back,' I continued. 'For the Tigers, or the Roos. One of those.'

'Not my teams.'

'The Tigers are all right,' Tony said. The cigarette was back in the corner of his mouth. One of his hands was stretched down the cobweb filled space between the couch and the exterior wall, the other one tugging the hair on the back of his head. His shrubby armpit looked wet and sticky. 'I knew a girl who was into that shit. Matched her bra and knickers on game day.'

'As in black and yellow?' Mitch said.

'I don't know. She never showed me.'

'Well if there are any faded red or discoloured white teams, consider me a fan,' I said.

'Any bare-chested, sign me up,' Tony said.

Mitch made a half-arsed attempt to kick at Tony's foot. 'I thought you went for the ones with skid marks down their backs,' he said.

'Yeah, they're all right too.' Tony grinned so wide it didn't make sense why the cigarette didn't fall from his mouth.

Those months I spent most of my time in that backyard couch. I really had nowhere else to go. Ron was all smiles when he came home. He'd started picking up tourist guides and road atlases and whatever he could find at the library that he dumped on the kitchen counter.

'One step closer,' he'd say before heading for the shower. Without getting up I made my hand look like an airplane taking off. When he turned away it swooshed back for a safe landing in my knee.

Ron went to bed early so usually we kept it quiet. Friends of Tony's came and went; there must have been at least twenty of them. They all had hair like him, as if they'd just come back from two months of isolation on an offshore oil rig. Their eyes looked tired, yet they never fully shut them, no matter how late we stayed up. When the sky went dark there were talks of starting a fire but we never got to it. A stray cat, we called her Jolly, kept climbing in from the street. We wiped an ashtray and filled it with water. She tramped all over us to get to it and if she was to stop and lay down it was always in the lap of Myra, the one who didn't enjoy company. Mitch had a 23-litre glass carboy in the hidden closet under the stairs and provided us all with drinks. The second or third week, Tony started handing me gifts. At first I didn't know what to say, but after a while I began saving them for later, usually until eight pm or so when the backyard was at its most beautiful. I'd pop it under my tongue and when Tony scoffed his I'd do the same and wait for the sun to hit the angle when the brick wall started to glow and shift from a sweet pumpkin to an underwater coral red. A smell of dust fell over us, grazing our pale palms—I made sure to hold them face up—slipping through the fingers to pick up whatever was left of the day. When it rose there was dew and there was vanilla and trust me when I say it was not only around us but inside us as well.

One morning we were still outside when I heard Ron coming down the stairs, ready for work. He didn't switch on the lights and remained a shadow, picking up his clunking tool belt and grabbing his lunch box from the fridge before leaving. If he saw us, he didn't let us know. He joined us on the

weekends, but never for too long and always too
bubbling with talks of scaffoldings and steel frames
and this guy John who once didn't just drop but rather
threw a bull pin over the Southbank promenade.

'Why on earth would he do that?' I said.

'The West Indies hat-trick. Imagine being
strapped sixty feet in the air when that news hit
you.'

When he left and Mitch went to get another
armful of beer Tony leaned over and pretended to
fall off the couch.

'That guy threw a ball and that other guy caught
it—tell me, what's now left to live for?'

I really started taking to Tony's gifts. He would dig
into his pocket and exclaim: 'Here comes Jolly!',
which had me doubled up with laughter.

'Get me some soft paws and a stingy attitude!'
I replied.

'Here's something stingy and soft for you,' he
said, pulling down his zipper to take out his dick.
It was all lumpy and hairy. Myra asked if she could
draw it, which she did. There he was, more pleased
than ever, a beer in one hand, a cigarette in the
other, and dangling from his fly, a soft dick all
mushy like an overripe kiwifruit. He started playing

with it but couldn't get it any harder and let it be.

'You're in the picture too,' Myra said to get me to stop howling, but even if I tried I couldn't straighten up.

Ron brought home a thick work on gothic architecture with a hideous gargoyle on the cover. I hid it under some magazines but the next day found it on my seat in the couch. I held it over my head just to drop it to the ground. The thud echoed over the laneway. It was still early afternoon.

'Hey Tony,' I said. 'Wanna fuck?'

Myra was right there, looking up from her journal. Tony nodded, all serious. We strolled up to his room which was the same size as ours but had a window facing the street. It was cooler on his side of the house so we slid under the doona. I kicked my shorts to the floor but kept the bra on. For once I pulled back his hair to see both his eyes. He took forever. There was a shelf with all the classics: Tolstoy, Dostoyevsky, Melville. Not just for show; they all looked well read. Afterwards he had a cigarette. I had one too. Ron would be home any minute, yet I stayed for another smoke and this time really took my time with it. I'd just put it away when I heard Ron coming through the front door and have a chat with Myra. Tony shook his head to get the fringe to cover his eye. I felt like I had a fever. I picked up my clothes, walked over to ours and laid down on the mattress, my belly still all sticky from Tony. Just when Ron entered the room I tossed a blanket over my groin.

'You all right?'

'Just tired.'

There was a dense and tangy ooze of sweat and genitals. It was all so obvious. Tony came out of his room with his belt still unbuckled and said hello.

'Go put a beer in the fridge and I'll be right down,' I said to Ron. He was halfway there when he turned around and came back, popping his big head through the door.

'You know what?' he said.

'What?'

'One step closer.'

Since Ron worked up until the day before our flight, he asked me to do most of the packing. I started folding my knickers but got distracted when Tony's friends arrived. With still a couple of days to go, Ron came home with flowers and a sponge cake. We had it by the kitchen table like a proper family.

'You cut your hair,' Ron said.

'Myra helped me.'

It had been sweltering for weeks. Ron thought his bronzed cheeks gave him a well-earned tradie look, but I couldn't help seeing a ten-year-old boy late for dinner, having chased sheep in the paddock the whole day. Mitch's forehead was all prickly with sweat; Tony and Myra looked cool. The cake tasted of butter and was soon gone from our plates.

'Where's your first stop?' Mitch asked looking at me. I looked at Ron.

'Trastevere, Rome. An apartment by the Tiber,' he said. 'Tiny. But two floors.'

'Beautiful. And from there to the City of Love?'

He looked at me and again I looked at Ron, who now was tapping his teaspoon on the tablecloth, seemingly reluctant to answer.

'Love, I like that,' Tony piped in.

'Yeah,' Mitch said, 'you can't say no to that.'

Ron kept hammering the same spot.

'Thanks again for this,' I said, not being entirely sure what I was referring to. Our time at Union Street was coming to an end, I knew that much. When I got up to clear the table, I noticed Jolly hiding behind Tony's legs. She didn't look like she wanted any affection. Still, I leaned down to offer her one of the plates.

**

On the shuttle bus I tried to talk to Ron. There was a wind outside that made the flags from the car dealers look all stiff and fake.

**

Our flat in London is nice. We have a squeaky oak door and a window overlooking a railway depot. In the early mornings you can sometimes see foxes balancing on the wooden fence.

When I think of my time on Union Street, it's all about the sunlight—its constant presence—and Tony, failing to keep his pale feet in its warmth. If he'd just stood up or moved the couch no more than an arm's length, he would've been right in it. So would've we all.

Recently, I've tried to tell myself that everything changes, that there might be a time to go back. Not that there's anything wrong with London. I must admit, I've grown to like it. And when it really comes down to it, isn't that what it's all about?

Things to Come

Charlotte Guest

1.

It was a day like this she'd feared the most. Felt it approach like some predatory animal, quietly and with a fixed gaze.

The air hung thick and close. It was too hot to make sense of difficult thoughts, to make plans.

She picked up the brush and ran it through her still-long hair. Thin, but long. Angel hair pasta, she thought. Always preferred angel hair to spaghetti anyway.

Still wearing her heeled shoes, she wandered into the kitchen, opened a drawer and took out a wad of Post-it notes. She took the pen from the side of the fridge and stretched the chord over the bench top.

Kettle, she wrote. *Keh-tal.* She paused, thinking, thinking herself back.

It was as if he'd had her surgically removed from his life. Cut out. It was too painful, he said, to pretend at friendship. Not when he still loved her. Not when he wanted to carry on and she didn't. *I feel we're at a fork in the road,* he said, cupping her hands in his, *you either decide to be with me or we end everything. I mean it. Everything. I can't have your shadow if I can't have you.*

She never could persuade him that it's okay to be unruly, that relationships are more innately liquid than he let them be. And yet she understood, like everyone understands, the need to alleviate pain.

In her parallel life he's been here all along. She comes home from the doctors and cries into his chest. She'd insisted on going alone. He tells her they'll work it out. He makes tea; they sit down. They Google what to do now. *You be the body and I'll be the brain,* he says. Gives her a smile.

She peeled the note off the pad and pressed it to the plastic tub. Stared at it.

1. *Fill the kettle with water*

117

2. *Place the kettle back onto the holder*
3. *Turn on the power*
4. *Flick the switch*
5. *Wait to boil*
6. *Light will turn off when ready*

The doctor was young, concerned. She wondered if she was his first.

'Olive. I have to tell you that—'

'I know.'

'There is medication.'

'I know.'

His kindness was irritating. He leant forward in a manner that was meant to say *I understand* but in fact said *I am not you and thank God for that.* She hated him.

There were many things she wished she didn't feel but did. She'd read a book that described mothers' guilt when their children contracted polio in the fifties. Felt they should have known. Felt they did know and ignored it. Failed. It was an oddly familiar feeling, even though she'd never had children.

How many years had passed? Forty? The last time she'd seen him he was walking through the departures gate, bound for Tasmania. They'd mapped every centimetre of each other's bodies in the years they were together. Seen the other change from adolescent into adult.

Don't call me please.

I understand.

Don't write to me.

I understand.

I love you.

I know. I love you too.

In the study she found the sticky tape and ripped off two even pieces, pressing her thumb to the serrated edge of the holder. She must tape the note to the kettle. Because, she thought, what if the Post-it came unstuck and fell to the floor so that the floor was labeled *Kettle* and the kettle nothing? Would she try to boil water on the lino? Was that possible? She pressed a flat palm to her forehead. Would it get that bad?

For months after he left she moved as if her self was curled up asleep inside the vessel of her body. But she didn't cry, or only rarely. Much less than she expected. There seemed to be no feeling in her face. *I need to learn to be alone,* she'd said. *You've always carried me with you, I don't know who I am without you. I need to find out.*

That's bullshit.

It's not bullshit.

I think you think it's bullshit too.
Think what you want.

The doctor had given her a sheet of paper. He asked her to fold it in half and put it on the floor next to the chair. She felt reduced to a child. Degraded. It reminded her of when she was young and called her grandmother a 'dribbler'. Dot, her mother's mother, had come to live with them after her grandfather died. She traipsed around the house singing out names Olive had never heard. Couldn't go to the toilet without her trying to find you. Dot put the iron in the fridge once, and Olive howled with laughter. Her mother went white, sent her away. Later she heard Dot crying.

Olive folded the paper and looked at the doctor. He waited. Stared at her intently. She had the sense he was telling her something but she didn't know what. Her hands felt heavy in her lap.

'Okay,' he said, marked something on his sheet. 'Okay.'

The light was beginning to fade in the kitchen. The yellow Post-it note glowed like it was radioactive. *Kettle. Keh-tal.* She went back to the mirror. *Keh-tal.* All words sound alien if you repeat them enough.

'Olive. Who do you want me to call?'

120

'What?'

'Who do you want me to call? I need to call someone.'

'Why?'

'Because you're going to need help. And company.'

She spread the brochures on the bench and felt their sleek, plastic coating. The granite is cold, she observed, the brochures are warm.

Outside the air was loosening. It was cool enough for the birds to perform their ritual jamboree, to sing in the night.

She approached the phone, pulled the address book from the sideboard. Forty years, or thereabouts. It was unlikely he had the same number. Or even a phone. Maybe he was deranged as well.

She punched in the digits. Felt her stomach rise to meet her throat. Felt her mind; felt it like it wasn't hers anymore. Like a growth that had gotten too big.

Don't ever call me. Or write.

I understand.

What was the purpose of this call?

It would be too much.

I know.

To tell him? To ask for help?

I love you.

What classifies as 'crawling back'? Does this qualify as self-centered?

I know. I love you too.

'Hello?'

'Matthew?'

'Yes. Who is this?'

There was a long pause. The light had gone from the kitchen. She could only hear, only think. She pressed her fingers to the bridge of her nose. Her eyes were damp, her cheeks and neck were damp. She caught her breath.

'... Olive?'

2.

The brochures hung limp in her hands, stuck to the sweat on her fingers. She felt flushed. There hadn't been five consecutive days over forty degrees since 1963, she thought. Heard it on the news this morning, on the way to her appointment. Committed it to memory: the last time there was five consecutive days over forty degrees was in 1963. Mouthed it to herself: 1963.

'Olive?'

A hand reached out and curled around her own. 'Take a look at them, shall we?'

Matthew took the first brochure, warm from Olive's hands, and laid it on the bench. Turned his back to her. 'Okay. Here we go: "for the newly diagnosed".'

Her hands felt heavy in her lap. She was suddenly aware of the processes of her mind, synapses firing, some hitting their targets, some not. She felt how her thoughts rose, morphed, slid away. The image of her grandmother, Dot, swam up from an old place. Dot, the wanderer. The crier. The gaping mouth, opening and closing, trying to convey what she was feeling. 'Like those clown heads at the fair,' Olive said to her mother, mouth wide, imitating, legs dangling off the high stool. Her mother didn't respond.

'It says here that we should identify some of the emotions you're feeling right now, to help process it.' Matthew swiveled to look at her, 'Can you describe how you're feeling?'

Olive looked at Matthew. How they'd aged. Clung to one another for forty-five years. And not always out of affection, but, at times, out of fear. To love the other but no longer be *in love*. To have known this from before they married.

She thinks of that night often. Remembers the heat from the fire, the uncomfortable seats. They had been short with one another for months. Tolerated each other's presence in the small apartment, tried to keep contempt from blooming like algae in the sink. Matthew suggested they take a weekend away to *reboot. Coupla stubbies and a crackin' sunset. That'll do it.*

The drive down was long and quiet. They listened to the radio until they drove out of range. Then they listened to the CDs stuffed in the glovebox. Then they listened to the sound of the car rolling over the highway.

At the campsite, after sundown, Matthew turned to Olive and clamped her hands between his. *I feel we're at a fork in the road,* he said. *Have been for a while. I feel you drifting away.* He lifted one hand to wipe his brow. *I just want us to be together. Partners.* He took the same hand and slid it into his pocket, drawing out a box. *It's either yes, or we end everything. I mean it, everything. If it's no, I don't want to be friends. I can't have your shadow if I can't have you.*

Olive never told her girlfriends the manner of his proposal. Always described the sunset, the fire, the sounds of the bush at night. That night she lay awake while he was sleeping, feeling the band around her finger with her thumb. She always felt she stumbled into her future, dazed and blinking.

'Olive? Give me some words, love, how are you feeling?'

That fucking horrid doctor, she thought, with his concerned expression. He smelt like paprika. Looked at her dumbly when she asked about voluntary euthanasia, mostly to spook him.

She told him about the Australian scientists who planned their suicides in accordance with their own mental and physical decline. They had specific criteria that, when met, indicated it was time to go. Inability to complete the quick crossword was one. Difficulty holding long conversations was another. Various physical tests. They were not medical scientists, these were just areas they decided were important. When both wife and husband began regularly failing their own tests they gathered the family together and declared their last week on earth. They organised a big meal with the finest produce they could afford. Their children stayed at the family home, talking long into the night with their parents. In the morning the scientists bid their daughters goodbye and asked them not to return to the house until late afternoon. Then they took out a series of prescription pills they had been hoarding and lay down on the bed. The daughters walked on the beach. Returned at five and called the ambulance.

The doctor opened his mouth. 'Olive, you know I can't—'

'I know.'

'There is medication.'

'I know.'

She'd driven home along the coast, insisted on going to the doctor's alone. How long until she wouldn't be able to drive? She loved the endlessness of the coastal road, its gentle winding, the car swaying like a boat. She selected a CD, pulled over at the lookout and sat for a long time, listening.

'Do you feel,' Matthew glanced at the brochure, 'despair?'

Outside the air was loosening. Birds were emerging, tentatively starting their evening jamboree. She remembered the same ritual at her mother's house; Dot on the verandah taking pleasure in the song of the garden. Her mother preparing dinner for three generations.

Olive rose from the chair and ambled into the study. She took a wad of Post-it notes and a pen and returned to the kitchen. Matthew watched her.

Went to say something, stopped.

Fridge, she wrote, and peeled off the note. Stuck it to the fridge.

Toaster. Phone.

'Olive.'

Microwave. Stove. Cutlery drawer.

She stopped. Looked at the note. Took it back. *Cutlery: utensils you eat with. Such as knives, forks, and spoons.*

'Olive, stop.'

Light switch. Cupboard. She opened the cupboard. *Cups. Saucers. Plates. Side plates. Milk jug. Wine glasses. Water glasses.* Closed the cupboard. Moved round to the window.

Kettle. Keh-tal. She sounded it out, wrapped her mouth around it. *Keh-tal.*

All words sound alien if you repeat them enough.

Keh-tal. Kettle. Kettle.

1. *Fill the kettle with water*
2. *Place the kettle back onto the holder*
3. *Turn on the power*
4. *Flick the switch*
5. *Wait to boil*
6. *Light will turn off when ready*

'Olive, please.'

She went back into the study and retrieved the sticky tape. Tore off two even pieces and taped the note to the kettle. Because… she thought. Because what if the note fell to the floor and she thought the floor was the kettle and the kettle some alien, unnamable appliance? What then?

What if she'd found the courage that night to say no? No to his possessiveness, his suffocating devotion. What if she'd stepped over him while he was sleeping and slipped away, into the bush, into a different life.

She had the unwelcome thought that her husband took a kind of pleasure in her diagnosis, because now, after forty years of marriage, she was fully his, fully in his care. A dependent.

Matthew stood behind her and rested a hand on the base of her neck. He felt it was cold and damp, felt her cheeks and nose were damp. Felt her collarbones, the ends of her angel hair.

'… Olive?'

Harbour Lights

Leslie Thiele

'Sure you don't want me to come with you? Not too late to find a sitter.'

'No,' Tanya had said, 'It's just a work thing. You'd be bored. I'm only going because I have to.' She needn't have worried. He had his eyes glued to the television, the remote a gun in his hand.

'You're right,' said Brian. 'A night out with my woman or a night in with my girl? No contest.'

'You look pretty, Mum,' Sasha looked up from the floor with a sleepy smile.

'Thanks, Sash. Not up too late now. See you both.'

'Have a good time,' Brian's voice followed her out into the cold. 'Drive safe.'

In the car she turned the music up loud and checked herself in the mirror. The glovebox sprung open and she slammed it shut automatically. She'd have to get it looked at, that was the third time now.

The road wound along the coast and over the estuary bridge. Across the bay, light swam in the still water reflecting the wealthier waterside areas. As teenagers, they'd cruised through there often enough, faces glued to the windows of the car. So she knew the way, even figured she knew the house. Helen and her husband had only been transferred here a few months ago. 'Sort of a housewarming,' Helen had said. 'Bring your husband.'

'Brian's busy Saturday,' she'd said without even the grace to blush. 'Some blokey thing.'

'Sure. Well, come alone anyway. It's nothing too fancy, we don't know many people yet. We can get to know each other better.'

'I'd like that.' And here she was, driving to the posh side of town in her best dress.

Outside Tanya fumbled with keys and wrap and bag, glad no-one was about to see her. Music leaked out from the lit windows. Jazz? At their last party Brian had insisted on playing all the old pub rock he loved so much. It was okay, secretly she liked it, danced easily enough on the prickly grass when she'd had a few. It wasn't like this though, this had class. She hadn't wanted Brian here. Didn't want this glamorous new boss to know how small-town they were.

When Helen arrived from head office, Tanya and the other girls had rolled their eyes at those impossible shoes and carefully tanned legs. Whispers suggested her husband was some bigwig in mining, lots of cash and a two-week roster. A few days later Helen took Tanya along on a trip on the south-west circuit to drum up extra business. *Two heads better than one and I could use someone giving directions around these backroads.* They discovered on the winding drive how much they had in common. Same age, married same amount of time, same likes and dislikes.

Tanya had talked about Sasha a lot and Brian not so much after hearing Helen praise her own husband. *Rob is such a go-getter ... If there's something he wants he just goes right out there and grabs it. He likes to win, that's for sure.* Not like Brian, the original Mr Live-and-let-live. After eight years, her husband's easy-going nature just felt like laziness. Brian had never been ambitious. She wondered what her life would be like with a *go-getter*, imagined the theatre instead of boozy backyard renditions of *Khe Sahn*.

Under the portico she surreptitiously checked her makeup before knocking lightly on the half-open door. 'It's just me.' A flutter of nerves, the sound of conversations already started. Helen came toward her dressed in something fluid and softly golden, her feet in strappy heels.

'Come on in,' she said. 'Rob's just organising drinks. Perfect timing.' She tucked Tanya's hand in the crook of her arm and led her toward the lit patio overlooking the bay, leaned in, whispering, 'I'm so glad you're here. It's all Rob's mates so far.'

Out on the deck Tanya was relieved to see she knew a few of the women from school drop-offs and didn't have to stand alone and awkwardly while Helen went off to find her husband.

'He's all right,' she was saying in response to a question about the new principal. 'I think he's got the school's best interests at heart.'

'Tanya! Excuse me, Kath.' It was Helen back again. 'Haven't introduced these two yet. Rob meet Tanya. Tanya this is my husband, Rob.' Tanya turned. She had her mouth open to greet and a hand already out to shake before it all fractured and froze on her.

She knew this guy.

If he'd thrown a punch to her stomach right

then she couldn't have been more shocked, more winded. He looked different. Polished up and tidy in his casual polo and chinos. He grabbed at her nerveless hand and pumped it up and down smiling maniacally at her, seemingly oblivious to her discomfort.

'Hi there, Tanya. Helen's told me how much easier you've made things for her.' His eyes were brown, she hadn't noticed that before. 'It's great to move somewhere new and find it's friendly. We've been lucky.'

'Lucky?' She sounded stupid, she felt stupid. She had always been stupid. Stupid, stupid, stupid. It ran through her mind over and over. Small wavy lines scrabbled at the edge of her vision, the decking felt miles below her. He leaned in toward her. She tried not to breathe in, felt she might be sick.

'I came here once years ago, football final,' he said quietly. 'Didn't think much of the place then. Full of bogans, like something out of *Deliverance*.' He chuckled at his own wit. 'Helen wasn't keen but we can make shitloads of money in a couple of years. Couldn't pass it up.' Tanya swallowed hard, pushed down the bile and wiped her sweaty hand on her dress as he went on. 'You lived here long?'

She stared at him. He didn't recognise her.

How could that be? Her heart set up an irregular flutter in her chest. She knew why. Because he'd been drunk. Stinking drunk. His visiting team had lost to theirs. All those city guys in their little town. *Fresh meat*, they'd giggled. She and her friends sitting on the sun-warmed sandstone wall, watching the game. Cheering like mad when the home team brought the trophy down even as they sloe-eyed the opposition.

Above the fireplace in their family room there was a photo—faded on one side from sunlight—of a muddied, youthful Brian being carried by his teammates, grinning like a loon. Tanya never looked at it. She always put the stereo on loud when she tidied in there, her face tight. Tiny and indistinct in the background, the opposing captain leant against the ablution block. Arms folded. Angry.

There had been a dried streak of mud on his forearm. She'd been thrilled when he'd singled her out at the end of season celebration. They'd had beer, and something else, something sweet and sharp. Lots of bright stars hanging. Wet kisses out by the deserted goalposts. Then suddenly rough. He'd turned her, pushed her down and torn at her. The sharp dewy blades of grass had scratched at her cheek. The awful *thwack thwack grunt* of him. And the hurting. Her tears leaking out, mouth open, soundless. Her outrage.

She'd waited, terrified and silent, in the darkness after he'd finished with her. Whimpered when he spat in her ear, *Tell your stupid mates I won the end game, bogan bitch.* His sudden laughter. Sliding footsteps. She'd waited there alone until she heard butcher birds start to stir in the gums. Spent ages looking for her knickers, strange sounds in her throat when she couldn't find them.

Her mum had given her a look over breakfast, hard-eyed, but she'd stared out the window at the sprinklers going around and around on the lawn and never had to answer the unspoken question there. Her skin sore from scrubbing. *Who used all the bloody hot water?* Her dad waiting by the car to go to church. *Teenage bloody girls!*

Later, in the hot sunshine she'd stood with her friends, laughing at the bloodstained pair of knickers hoisted on the flagpole outside the grounds. *Whose could they be?* they'd asked, looking around at each other. *What sort of slut would let a boy do that?* Her cheekbones hurt like glass. She'd worn the shame of it flaming like a brand on her soul. She'd never said a word. Not one.

Not even when Brian playfully flipped her over

once and she'd come up screaming, swinging at him. Beside herself with fury, fractured words all snotty and glottal. Still she hadn't told him, just pushed it way way down and sobbed herself into a numb stupor, let him pull the blankets up around her shoulders and slept and slept.

'You want to talk?' he'd said when she'd woken.

'No.'

'You know you can trust me don't you, Tan?' Scratching meaty fingers through his reddish hair. 'Whatever it is. I've got your back. It's part of the deal.' She'd turned away in silence, unwilling, unable.

She thought of Sasha, so small beside her father there on the couch tonight. God, if anything like that ever happened to her, Brian would kill them. Just kill them. Unless Sasha was like her and she never said. Unless silence gave them some tacit approval. Then they'd be just like this guy. Standing here in his casuals in his big fancy house like he'd never been on the wrong side of the line. Because she, Tanya, had let him.

'You okay?' he said now. 'You don't look so great.'

'You bastard,' she said.

'Pardon?'

'I said, *you bastard*, you deaf fuck.' She felt people turn and stare, saw Helen reach out, face swerving from party smile to shock. 'You make me sick.'

'Hey, lady, um … Tanya? I don't know what you're on about but I think you'd better calm down.'

Her eyes were so wide she could feel the night air brush at her tears. 'I was fourteen, you sicko. Fourteen!'

Helen grabbed at her forearms and held them hard, forcing her to turn.

'Tanya? What is the matter with you?'

'Ask him what happened, Helen, what he did. When I was fourteen. On the school oval.' Saying it out loud was like vomiting. Her mouth a rush of sour.

'Jesus.' She heard Rob laugh uneasily behind her. 'She's crazy.' Tanya saw something shift behind his smile.

'Tanya. I think you should leave now, honey. Something's upset you.' Helen was all conciliation, eyes round with concern. 'Can I phone someone for you?'

Tanya stared at her. 'Upset me? You think something has upset me? Damn right it has,' she pointed. 'He has. Your fucking husband has.

Fucking ...' She could feel hysterical laughter rising in her throat. 'Oh, Jesus,' she choked. 'Oh, Jesus what am I even saying?' People were moving toward them, faces confused. Her hands were shaking when she grabbed her bag. She shoved it under one arm and pointed at him with the other. 'You know! You *know* what you did, you bastard.'

Rob turned toward his friends, hands up in the air and surprised eyebrows. 'Sorry, folks, she's one crazy bitch. I've never seen her before in my life.' Already they were looking at him differently.

She made her way stumbling out of the house and across the lawn to her car. Faces gaped behind her, a muffled rush of chatter starting up. Helen's voice shrill: 'What is she talking about, Rob? What's going on?' Tanya didn't hear his answer. Didn't care what he said. Her fledgling friendship with Helen was over. It didn't matter anyway. Nothing did.

In the car, her fumbling angry hands had to turn the key twice before the engine caught, the tyres scattered gravel as she pulled out from the drive. Around the bay she drove, over the bridge, the harbour lights glittering still on the water. She drove fast, before the shame could catch up with her and the silence reach back up her throat.

On the high road she pulled into a parking bay

overlooking the beach. Moonlight rode rippling whitecaps into shore. Tanya stood at the top of the weathered steps leading down toward the sand. The breeze was cool coming off the ocean, strands of hair caught in the wet of tears which would not stop. She pulled her wrap close around her shoulders and wiped her face with one end, careless of makeup. Tasted salt. Clouds scudded across the night sky, stars winking in and out at her. She sat on the top step and stared at the glittering sea. No-one knew where she was. Nothing could touch her here.

There was time still to rewind what she had said tonight. Plead hormones or something. Nobody wanted trouble, not really. She'd known that even back then. Her mother had never asked about her rash-flushed face, the bruise on her jaw. Curiosity killed the cat.

Time spun out and away drifting into the giant sky and she had been here an hour, two. Her fingers were cold, the wrap damp from the sea air. Her teeth chattered. No definitive plan of action presented itself. Big enough to be named a city, this was still a small town at heart. Her mother's friends still spoke to her as though she was the child they once knew. Everyone was related to someone and secrets were whispers that slithered like serpents through the very fabric of the town.

She felt empty, scoured out and strangely peaceful. Home. She just wanted to be home. All she had to do was drive a few miles west and kiss her little girl goodnight, slide under the blankets with Brian and keep her mouth shut. Life could just go on. It was a fair bet Helen and Rob would leave town at some stage earlier than planned. She'd seen fear slide underneath the muscles in his face. He wouldn't want to risk another encounter. It would all go away and she could go back to being just Tanya. The path of least resistance beckoned to her in the quiet night air.

She fished the keys from her bag and made her way back up the steps to the car, bone-tired. She turned the key and backed the car, swung it round to face the road. Hit the blinker for home. The glovebox sprung open, she hit it shut. It sprung open again, and then again. Each time she slapped it shut. And again. And again.

'Stop it,' she said aloud, annoyed now. And again. Open, slap, shut, open. 'Just stop it, for fuck's sake!' Open. Slap. Open. She slammed her hand hard against the dashboard, stinging her palm though the lid had long jammed. 'Stop it! Stop.

Just *STOP*.' The tears had started up again, her face rubber and liquid. 'I said no. I said *NO!*'

The word echoed to silence. Her hands couldn't seem to get a grip on the wheel, clenching and releasing in waves of anger and uncertainty. She was away from herself, watching the woman in the car, wondering what she would do.

The indicator ticked loudly, flashes of green against her skin. *Just leave it, Tanya.* In seven years' time her daughter would be fourteen. Still such a child even then. Would the sleeping dogs still be lying then? *Just leave it alone.* She looked back toward town. They had a twenty-four hour manned police station now they were officially a city. They'd laughed about it over the breakfast talkback, her and Brian. What on earth would they have to do in the wee hours other than chase a few hoons around in cars? Here in this back-end place where nothing ever happened? *This*, she thought, turning the steering wheel to the right. They would have *this* to do.

Dependence Day

Sophie McClelland

He awoke to the familiar nagging pain agitating his knuckles. Keeping his eyes closed for the precious remaining moments of rest, he began to rub the tenderer joints of his right hand with his left, though the painful sensation picked away at it too. When he could no longer bear to lie there in the dark, as more limbs succumbed to their aches, he opened his eyes and looked at the empty pillow beside his own, a force of habit still yet to die despite her having been dead for over twenty years. There she had once been, every night and every morning for decades. He closed his eyes again and saw her hair—not as it was towards the end, but how he remembered it from when they were first married—a glowing nest of honey-coloured curls that seemed to catch and hold the morning light before refracting it towards his love-lost eyes.

How cold the bed had been without her. It was this that had taken him by surprise. He'd expected his ears would strive to hear her voice again, that his eyes would long for a glimpse of her, and that his skin would turn numb from its solitude. But he hadn't given a thought to how, at night, his whole body would feel chilled without the warmth of her beside him. Of course, he had done all the practical things—hot water bottle, a pillow beside him—but still he felt the chill of loss to his bones as he carried on without her.

Carry on, though, he did. It was something he'd always managed to do. Even in the very bleakest of circumstances, as a prisoner of war in Malaysia, starving, ravaged by the malaria and other wretched diseases that had invaded his exhausted and emaciated body. Even then he'd clung to the hope of surviving with a quiet yet fierce tenacity, reminding himself he was lucky to have survived up to that point anyway, a coin toss having been the deciding factor over which doctor would be sent to which hospital (he'd called heads and, as luck would dictate, it was heads and he'd picked the field hospital outside the city). Two months later the other doctor was killed when his hospital was stormed by Japanese troops who'd spared none.

He sighed and turned his head back, staring at the ceiling as he pondered for some moments how much his eyes had seen over the years and how frustrating it was that like his legs they seemed to be giving in to age more quickly than the rest of him. He blinked hard, pushing the thoughts away, and set about getting out of bed—not an easy task at the age of one-hundred-and-two. Each careful movement came with a bone creak. 'At least you've still got your marbles, Grandad,' Helena would offer each time she saw him wince from the effort of getting out of his chair. 'Still got my marbles,' he'd repeat with a nod.

He worked his way gradually up into a seated position, enjoying the warmth of the covers a little longer while he smoothed out the duvet cover before him. The sheets, originally a bold floral print, were faded now, but because they had been Kate's favourite, it was this set and another that he insisted the cleaner alternate between, despite there being several new sets that Helena had bought him, sitting in the linen cupboard.

When he was ready, he gripped the edge of the duvet and deftly pulled it off his legs in a sweeping arc motion that had been honed to perfection over the years. It took a bit more effort to swing his legs off the bed, but after that his feet soon found his slippers and, with a momentum-adding push from his hands, he was up.

It wasn't yet light at this time of the morning. He woke earlier and earlier these days—a result, he knew, of indulging in an afternoon nap—but nodding off in his chair was one of the few luxuries he afforded himself during his structured days. He switched on the landing light as he made his way towards the stairs for the slow and deliberate descent. He would stay downstairs all day, shaving and dressing in the bathroom down there to avoid any unnecessary trips back up, but even so it was hard going on his knees, whose efforts were at least still proving victorious against the threat of a stair lift—or worse, a home—another looming dread towards the loss of his carefully guarded independence.

At the bottom of the stairs he stopped for his customary pause, collecting and steadying himself with one hand holding firmly to the smooth wooden top of the banister. 'Right, then.' He shuffled to the kitchen and set the kettle on to boil for a cup of tea. He reached for his mug and began to whistle as he grasped the fine china, enjoying its smooth, cool touch on his pained hand. His whistle was not the usual type blown through puckered lips, but a softer, more rasping sound created from setting his teeth almost together, holding his tongue back a little and blowing the air over it against his teeth, altering the pitch of the sound by moving his lips around. *Sissis–sossoo, sissis–sossoo.* The repetitive mantra kept the silence of the kitchen at bay once the tea was made and followed him down the hall to his study, continuing to soothe him as he turned the lamp on and drew back the curtains. Soon the meagre light of the early morning would assist in illuminating the room and its shelving-clad walls jam-packed with books and papers.

He sat at his desk, took a sip of scalding tea, licked the side of his lip and picked up the journal he had begun reading yesterday afternoon. It was the latest volume from the Society for Allergy & Clinical Immunology and would take him at least another day or two to finish. He stopped whistling as soon as he began reading—so absorbed was he by the subject. He had found the workings of medicine fascinating ever since his boyhood, and the ensuing decades had done nothing to dampen his enthusiasm for the subject. Quite the opposite; in fact, his distinguished career was still very much alive. He'd found that retirement had not suited him and had returned to work after two failed attempts to stop, deciding after the second time that he'd continue for as long as possible. Even now, a centenarian, he gave lectures when invited and saw a few of his long-term patients.

**

Helena stared at the froth topping her coffee, wondering if she'd switched off her straighteners. She dipped her spoon into the longest frond of the decorative espresso-stained fern atop the latte and stirred with a slow deliberate motion, watching it melt into the coffee as she tried to still her mind into recalling the precise moments of when she'd finished and put them down. Other thoughts sped through —*Had she packed fruit with the girls' sandwiches? She must text Hayley with an RSVP to Alfie's party* —and scattered her already messy memories. She knew she'd spent longer straightening her hair this morning as it had dried wet overnight and was at its curliest, most irritating when she woke, so she'd hurried through her makeup application before having to dash downstairs to break up the fight that had escalated in the kitchen over who'd used up the last of the bread.

On the drive to school, the girls had reminded her that it was Friday (time was always running away from her), which meant she'd be meeting Claire for a quick coffee—their weekly treat—before heading to the supermarket for Grandad and fitting in a bit of work before it was time to collect Maisie and Ellen.

'Where has the week gone?' Claire smiled as she plopped down in the chair opposite and wrapped both hands around her mug of herbal tea. 'I could've killed Dave this morning. There he was, feet up, chewing his cereal and watching the news while I hared about the place, trying to get the kids fed, dressed and lunchboxes ready, half-dressed and hungry myself. Thought I was going to implode. He's lucky I had this to look forward to.' She raised her mug with a wink.

'I know.' Helena rolled her eyes and took a sip of coffee before continuing, 'They just don't get it. I'm so fed up with James but I don't have the energy to even tell him anymore. Nothing changes and I just get told I'm a nag.' She shrugged. 'Anyway, there are other things to worry about—like whether I've left my bloody straighteners on.' She did a mock head bang on the table.

'Oh, not again! You didn't last time so I'm sure you haven't this time. Drink your coffee and tell me about your week.'

As they chatted and laughed at more 'brain-frazzled' (as they liked to call it) lapses, Helena could feel some of the tightness across her shoulders beginning to ease. She always felt better for catching up with Claire, her friend since she'd been expecting Maisie. They had waddled through the park together, cradling their bowling-ball bumps, talking excitedly about what was to come and bonding over the less widely shared details of pregnancy. Their time together was always easy, even with the four kids in tow, and today was no exception.

'How's your grandad?'

'Oh,' her eyes darted to her mobile, which lay face-up beside her cup, 'he's okay, I think.' She paused. 'You know, sometimes I worry about him more than I do about Dad.'

'That's understandable, Lena.'

'Is it?' Her eyes looked up and searched Claire's for affirmation, relieved when she found it.

'Of course. Your dad is being looked after by kind people, in a nice home ...'

'And he's so far gone now that there's not a lot anyone can do.'

'Your grandad is almost the opposite: a still-brilliant mind trying to coax on a body that's, well, really old. Is he still insisting on staying in the house?'

'Yep. He always says to me when I try to bring it up, "Not yet, love, not yet." I don't want to push him, but I'm worried he won't be able to manage for much longer. It's those stairs. If he was in a bungalow, it would different. I wish he'd sold the house and moved into something more age-friendly after Nan died.' She stopped for a second to sip at her coffee, taking the opportunity to look up and rapidly blink back unexpected tears that had pooled in her eyes.

Claire noticed but didn't say anything.

**

Over lunch—a ham sandwich and packet of salt-and-vinegar crisps (they played havoc with his dentures but it was Friday, and on Fridays he had crisps)—he thought about Jack. They had enjoyed a regular weekly lunch together, sometimes at the pub but usually here at Frank's house. Jack had been fifteen years younger than Frank, and they'd both quietly assumed that as the younger man he would outlive Frank; silly really, to make such assumptions after all the years spent bearing witness to the indiscriminate nature of death, but Jack had always been the picture of health—a lithe, sprightly man with a warm smile and mischievous eyes. He had walked along the seafront every day of his retired life and was not plagued by the aches and pains that besieged Frank. They had worked together for years, enjoying intellectual sparring bouts between collaborative efforts at the hospital. One morning Jack had simply not woken up. A death that the man himself would have chosen, and one in a long line of deaths that Frank had lived through. Yet another friend who'd bitten the dust before him. He didn't usually let his thoughts linger for too long upon such things, but today was Friday and, he supposed, Jack was someone with whom he had spent much time over the years.

Turning one-hundred had been something of an anticlimax. His family had bubbled with excitement as he'd edged towards his century. The birthday cards he received in the years leading up to the big day all shared the sentiment that he wouldn't have to wait much longer for his telegram from the Queen. But on the day itself, after the obligatory celebrations of cake and candles, hats and back pats, he'd stared down at the much-heralded telegram in his hand and felt underwhelmed. What now? He'd got there. He'd reached a hundred. What was there to wait for now? Just the inevitable, he thought, pursing his lips and reminding himself how lucky he was to still be in his own home, still working and still structuring his days as he saw fit. It was a lot more than those poor buggers in the nursing homes had. He might be lonely, but he was free—well, independent at least.

As he picked up another crisp his thoughts moved to Helena. Those worried eyes that so deeply searched his own when she asked how he was. Her anxiousness was palpable. He'd watch as her eyes darted about the place as she clutched her mobile phone and periodically held it up to check she'd not missed anything, occasionally tapping some reminder into it and mumbling apologies to him as she did so, while he tried to engage her in conversation. She had such beautiful curls—just like her mother and grandmother—but for too long now she'd ironed them straight, the style hanging flat and heavy around her face, as if taking on the cares that weighed upon her. Such a contrast to how, when she'd been young and carefree, those lightweight curls had delightfully bounced about her shoulders, twirling, whenever she laughed. He longed to see her like that again.

**

Helena was at the supermarket, checking the time on her phone. She was running late and would have to get a move on if she was going to get some work done at home before picking up the girls and delivering the groceries to Grandad. As she marched towards the ready-meals aisle, trying to manoeuvre the cumbersome and uncooperative trolley around the corner, she thought of his voice. He had such a calm, measured way of speaking that belied all that he had been through: years spent in a POW camp, which he had only begun speaking of in his nineties; losing his wife, his daughter, and so many of his friends. He was remarkable. A product of a hardy generation. It soothed her to listen to him and, although there never seemed enough time, she'd always linger to hear him talk more.

**

Later that afternoon she took the girls with her to deliver his shopping. He seemed well, she could hear him regaling the girls with a tale about a fishing trip he'd taken to the Lakes while she'd re-stocked the fridge. The story was an old favourite of hers and she smiled while she ran a cloth around the kitchen.

**

He'd enjoyed the visit from Helena and the girls and had slept well the night before, rising a little later this morning. He switched on his portable radio to tune in to his usual Saturday morning program, holding on to it as he made his way towards the stairs. He'd continue listening over breakfast and then get back to reading the journal, which he should get finished before lunch at the rate he was going. He began the descent, painstakingly lumbering one foot after the other down each step. His knees clicked with every movement and he had to breathe deeply to combat the pain that reared with each downward jolt.

A few steps from the bottom, something happened; he was hit by a wave of dizziness that weakened his grip on the banister and set him off balance. Before he knew it, he'd fallen.

**

For several moments he lay at the bottom of the stairs on his side, registering the pain that seared through his hip and down his leg in spasms as he stared numbly at the radiator tap before him. He studied the gleaming chrome and its regular indentations, and started to cry. Silently. Each tear took its time brewing to fruition before sliding down his face, gathering speed as they mingled to form a steady stream that dripped onto the floor, forming a filigree of dark droplets on the carpet.

**

Two hours later Helena unlocked his front door, calling in to fetch the stuffed toy that Ellen had left yesterday. She stepped into the hallway and sang out her usual greeting as she shut the door behind her, stopping abruptly as she turned back around and saw her grandfather lying in a heap at the bottom of the stairs. Alive, thank goodness, but hurt. As she rushed to him, mobile in hand ready to ring for an ambulance, she looked at his face and noticed something she had never seen before. His cheeks were wet. He was crying. He never cried. Not when he lost Nan; not even when he'd buried his daughter.

**

It had run out. The luck that had stayed with him all these years. The hope and determination that had carried him through even the bleakest hours at the POW camp. *She'll put me in a home, she'll put me in a home*, he thought over and over until he could no longer bear to think, and closed his eyes.

Ms Lovegrove

Emily Paull

I almost forget the play now.

No, I'm lying. How could I forget?

If I hear the name, it's like I've been slapped. It was the first play I ever starred in, back in university. Our state had an illustrious university theatre program. They only took fifteen people every year. I was eighteen years old, straight out of high school—a place where I had been told time and time again that I was 'exceptional'. But at university I found myself surrounded by people who were 'exceptional'; people who broke into monologues as they spoke to you outside the classroom, people who sang Broadway hits in the cubicle next to yours

in the ladies' room, people who thought knowing
Shakespeare plays off by heart was a party trick.
They were thinner than I was, most of them, and
shorter and made me feel like a clumsy giant, or a
giraffe in roller skates.

I turned up to my first lecture and placed
myself in the very centre of the front row. She
walked in without looking at any of us and put her
notes on the lectern. Ms Polly Lovegrove her name
was; we all knew her already. She'd been in a long-
running television soap opera, and starred in all the
local plays going back to before I was born. Taking
off her glasses, she stepped past the lectern and
peered at us.

'Most of you,' she said, then paused for effect, 'will
never be on *Home and Away* or *Packed to the Rafters*.
You will most likely not be on television at all during
your careers, which will be short. You *may* never even
get to a level of competency which will see you on stage
with an amateur theatre company. Statistically, half
of the people in this room will have dropped out by
the time you are supposed to be graduating. These
are the facts, and you must accept them now, and be
willing to work hard to prove me wrong.'

I rolled the way she said 'amateur' around in my
mouth. 'Amater.' 'Amater.'

She continued, 'In this course you will undertake no fewer than six major productions, one a semester, each with a different director. You will be competing for roles with every other person in this room. I'm telling you now that the people who come to see these performances will be the people hiring you—or not hiring you—after university.'

She did not smile, or end with comforting words, and the room was so silent I had to turn and make sure there were other students behind me. My palm left a sweaty mark on my notepad. Then Ms Lovegrove clapped her hands to signify that she was done with the preamble and launched into the lecture.

After class, I headed to the library, where a quick Google search on Ms Lovegrove revealed that she was the former director of Banksia Theatre, the largest company in the State, with the most sponsors. I'd seen several of her plays, *The Tempest*, and a production of *Death of a Salesman* in which Willy Loman had been played by a red-haired woman. A few years previously, she had 'stepped down from the helm' and taken up teaching, citing 'a commitment to nurturing the State's young talent' and a 'desire to reinvigorate

Perth culture'. As an actress, she'd played Viola, Caligula and Lady Windemere, but the role of Polly Lovegrove, nurturer, was to be 'her toughest role to date'.

The following Monday, during my first workshop, I experienced something a little like the fluttering stomach-butterflies of love as Ms Lovegrove swanned into the room in a pair of tailored black pants and high heeled boots.

'I won't be taking attendance in this class,' she said, taking a spot in the centre of the dark, bare room and waving her hands to indicate she wanted us to come closer. 'You know if you are here or not. By the end of the semester, I will remember the names of those of you who have worked hard, as well as those who have earned my ire. I can tell you from previous years that students who do not make themselves memorable do not go on to do well.'

I could feel my heart beating behind my breast. My skin was warm. Like everyone else in the room, I was dressed in black stretch pants and a dark singlet, but unlike everyone else, my body was curvy and stood out. Not one of us was wearing shoes, though we had not been told to take them off. I chucked my chin higher, and imagined that she was talking only to me. Ms Lovegrove clapped her hands and we began our warm up.

She had us walk about the room with no specific direction, asking us to feel aware of our bodies, and to lead with our toes or our belly buttons or our foreheads. She had us lie on the floor and meditate, and when one of the boys appeared to fall asleep, she took up the blackboard ruler and smacked it against the floor by his ear, causing all fifteen of us to jump to attention.

By the end of class, I was covered in chalk and dirt from the floor. With a sigh, Ms Lovegrove looked at the stainless steel wall clock above the door and said, 'That is all.'

Fifteen pairs of tired feet scrambled for the sides of the room to pick up bags and shoes. Ms Lovegrove held up a hand. We froze. 'Wait.'

With a manicured fingernail, she pointed at four of us: myself and three other girls. 'Stay behind.'

A ball of salty tears rose in my mouth. The four of us stood as the lucky eleven who had escaped attention moved past us with their heads down and burst into the fading sunshine outside. She waited until the door had closed behind them again to speak.

'Our production this semester is going to be

A Streetcar Named Desire. All four of you displayed a level of focus which impressed me. You seem well-presented enough and you have the kinds of faces which I can work with.'

Ms Lovegrove turned and went to the curtain covering the back wall. She pulled it aside with the ring of hooks, revealing rows of costumes, a set of flats for painting sets on, wooden chairs and buckets of half-used paint and brushes, as well as a bookshelf containing playbooks. A contemplative finger scanned the shelf and came to rest at 'W' for Williams. She removed four copies and stood holding them out.

'After tomorrow's class you will each audition for Blanche.'

I looked at the script and then at the other girls. In my mind, I had the strangest notion that the part was already mine. I smiled at Ms Lovegrove, waiting to catch her eye. Eventually she did look at me, but her face was blank, mouth downturned like that of a giant koi.

The next day, she chose our scenes for us, a different one for every girl, and we auditioned in order of our appearance in the play. I was third.

I felt the world go still as I waited. I felt

the boredom of the two girls who had already auditioned and the nerves of the girl who had not. Ms Lovegrove was seated on a pillow with her legs tucked under her. She was tapping her lower lip with a fountain pen. I took a deep breath and began.

'Thank you,' she murmured, her voice the slice of a pair of scissors in fabric. I stopped with my mouth still open.

'There's more to the scene.'

'I have seen enough.'

I dropped the papers to my side. 'But the others got to finish their scenes, I haven't even got through one line!'

She glanced at me over her cat-like spectacles, and I am sure I saw her smile. 'You'd like to finish?'

'I'd like the chance.'

She glanced at the other two girls who had already performed. 'I saw more of Blanche in you in those six sentences than I saw in these two put together. The part is already yours. But by all means, continue.'

The room was so silent that the sound of her pen in her notebook was like the murmur of a waiting audience. I swallowed the spittle that had gathered around my tongue. 'The part is …'

Ms Lovegrove rolled her eyes. 'Yes, it's yours.

Don't get excited yet, you've merely been cast. The hard work is now ahead of you.'

The final girl, the one who had not yet auditioned raised her hand. Ms Lovegrove slid her glasses up on her nose. 'Yes, I know I didn't see your audition yet. Do you want to read for Stella? Will that prevent your complaints?' The girl withdrew her hand. Ms Lovegrove glanced back to me, her mouth twisting. 'What are you still doing here? Go.'

I turned and went as commanded, clutching my script in my left hand even while I was collecting my bag with my right, and I did not once look back.

She had cast me, but she did not like me.

I walked too heavily, I was too tall and curvy, and difficult to costume. There were costumes in storage already which had been used in every other production of *Streetcar* the university had ever done, but they sat above my knees and wouldn't zip up. Until I'd been to this school I had never thought of myself as overweight but the experience of having a teacher pinch at the rolls of skin which bunched under the sides of my bra was humbling. As she attempted to do up one of the dresses, she muttered, 'There's simply not enough time to lose all this extra padding.' A special appointment was made with the students from the costume design program. I was expected to give up my evenings until the costumes were complete.

She was always watching me as I rehearsed. When I looked at her from my point on the stage, Ms Lovegrove's lips were working back and forth as she sat across the room, her nose crinkled with distaste.

To the boys in our class she was nurturing, almost inappropriately so. She pressed her body up against theirs as she showed them how to stand, how to sit, how to lean over a poker table. There were surprisingly few women in the cast, just myself and Eleanor, who was playing Stella, and a girl named Lynne, who had been cast as Eunice. Only Eleanor was from the original quartet who'd auditioned. She was the last girl, the one who'd not been asked to read. The girls who had read, Dawn and Rachel, had been relegated backstage and given non-speaking parts. There were no understudies. The show would go on the way Ms Lovegrove had cast it.

A visiting actor came to speak to the class. Toby Duprie had been Ms Lovegrove's first pupil, her protégé, her discovery. When he was warm and friendly to us, and gave numerous smiles to the girls, it seemed to drive Ms Lovegrove mad. Her arms crossed her body with such ferocity, I thought she might squeeze her own torso off.

The final dress rehearsal was upon us too soon. She called us in to work scene by scene. Scene Ten was myself and a boy named Phillip, who was to be Stanley. It was a short scene. I had been costumed in a shiny negligee and a matching dressing gown trimmed with feathers. My hair was wrapped and in curlers. My face was heavily made up. I could hear the burr of conversation backstage where the rest of the class was passing the time.

'We're going to run this scene with everything we've got!' Ms Lovegrove said from her chair in the back of the auditorium. She was wearing a trilby hat and her eyes were shielded. Phillip nodded, his thick black glasses sliding down his face. As he pushed them up the bridge of his nose, Ms Lovegrove scoffed. 'For heaven's sake, take those off. Do you think Stanley Kowalski wears Clark Kent glasses? He's a brute, he's a man's man. If he experienced any short sightedness, he would be far too proud to say a damned thing.'

I could see Phillip's hands shaking as he removed the specs. My own hands were trembling from the cold in the room. I took my seat on the brass bed to one side of the set and wished with all my might that the cold tea in the bottle on the nightstand was really bourbon.

Phillip made to go backstage, to put his glasses away. 'Where are you *going*, Phillip?'

'I need to put in my contacts, it will only take a...'

'We don't have time for you to put in your contacts, you will just have to do it without them.'

He nodded and walked straight into the empty doorframe on set. She signalled for the lights to go up. We began. We had almost made it through the scene, when ...

'Stop, stop stop!'

We stopped and stood blinking in the lights, looking for her. Her shoes clopped on the boards as she made her way to the front of the stage.

'I'm not feeling the fear in you, Nicole, I'm not feeling like Blanche is terrified of Stanley. And Phillip, I'm not feeling that Stanley is enraged enough to rape Blanche yet.' She looked at us, considering for a moment. 'You need to wrench off her dress.'

My hands flew involuntarily across my chest. 'What?'

Ms Lovegrove raised her eyebrows. 'You won't be naked, Nicole, it will just be your breasts.'

Phillip had gone the colour of tomato soup and was choking. I glared at her.

'It's too late to give the part to one of the others. Do it, Nicole.'

I bared my teeth and nodded dumbly, shaking the tension out of my shoulders. Phillip looked as if he would faint.

'Phillip, take it from "Come to think of it— maybe you wouldn't be bad to—interfere with". Say it like you're angry with her, like you want to push her down into the floor and make her shut her filthy whore's mouth!'

I shivered. Was it Blanche she was talking about, or me?

Phillip swallowed and nodded to me, and I nodded back. He delivered his line.

Ms Lovegrove jumped up like a spectator at a dog fight. 'Now, Phillip!' she cried. 'Pull the strap until it breaks, push her onto the ground and press your knee into her back! Wrench the dress up over her head! Roll her over!'

He lunged, teeth bared. His hand was cold as it closed around the top of my arm, pulled me roughly from the bed and onto the floor. His other hand was roaming inside the dressing gown for the strap. He found it and pulled it. He did as he was told, rolled me and pinned me, and pulled the material over my head. I screamed. I screamed in real terror as the silk slipped over my mouth and momentarily gagged me. My breasts sprung free, pressed into the sandy floor of the set. I didn't dare look. We kept going. I took the bottle and smashed it over the edge of the table, harder than I had intended.

'So I could *twist the broken end in your face*!' I hissed through my tears. My voice was a ragged stream of breath. Phillip skittered back.

He lunged at me, grabbed me by the waist as I struggled, hoisting me over his shoulder, my bared breasts hanging free towards the ground as I screamed and cried.

'Keep going, Phillip!' cried the disembodied voice of Polly Lovegrove. 'Drop her forcibly on the bed. Climb on top of her. Rear up. Beautiful! Unzip your trousers! Now press yourself between her legs. Slower! Dim the lights.'

The room became quiet as the lights went out. All I could hear was my own sobbing, and Phillip's heavy, ashamed breathing. He hurried off me, zipping his pants as he went, and tripping over the edge of the bed. The broken glass crunched under his shoes. I hurried to pull the bed's sheets around me before the lights were brought back up.

She was standing by the edge of the stage.

'Much better!' she cried, applauding. She was looking at Phillip, but he'd angled his body towards the wall. 'Are you all right, Phillip?'

He sniffed and swiped at his eyes. 'Yes.'

I could feel the rivulets of snot hanging down the sides of my mouth. I couldn't hold back anymore. The fear, the shame, the shock, it all came out and I wailed like a child.

Her lip twitched, and she said, 'Pull yourself together, Nicole.'

We ran it that way on opening night, and every night after that. I reminded myself that the crowd was made up of people who could determine my future, the casting directors and the agents of every company in the city. I did not invite my mother.

On closing night, as we broke down the sets and swept the broken glass from the floor, I saw her for the last time. She was standing by the exit door, supervising the transport of the set pieces into the truck. I had walked over to her before I knew what was happening. She turned and she looked at me impatiently.

'I guess I just want to know why,' I said. I folded my arms across my chest.

She snorted. 'You wouldn't understand.'

'Let me decide if I understand or not.'

Ms Lovegrove sighed and she threw her hands up in exasperation. 'You young women, you come through this program and you all think you're going to get to where I got, and it's going to be like a fairy tale. It's not a fairy tale. This is an industry where to make it, and I mean to *really* make it, as a woman, you have to do some despicable things.'

'Then you should be helping us to change that. You're our teacher. It's your job.'

'No. My job is to help you realise that the world is sometimes a dirty, ugly place. I don't have to help you students, and I especially don't have to like you. You did well tonight, Nicole, because I helped you access something real. You'll be thanking me for the rest of your professional life.'

My lip curled, and I fought the urge to spit at her feet. 'I think you're wrong about that,' I said.

In the half-light of the empty stage, she looked much older than usual. 'I don't give a damn what you think,' she said.

As I left the theatre, my whole body began to shake, and I fought the urge to cry.

Better Than the Farm

Miriam Zolin

I know the street you live on. I used to live near there myself when I first came to Sydney. Dog shit on the streets and no good long grass to wipe your boots on, get them clean. The noise at night from trucks on Parramatta Road. I used to think about all the things I did that brought me here. All the little decisions. The twists and tiny turns that had me lying awake so far from big skies and wide plains.

Not for you to worry about though. We all have our own stories. Where are you heading? North Sydney, you say? Well, you'll have to cross the harbour from here.

Here's what I'd do.

Catch the bus to Wynyard Station, just around
the corner there. They're only every twenty minutes,
so if you've just missed one you might want to walk
down to Broadway and catch a bus from there. Be
careful though. The buses are nearly all full by the
time they get to Broadway. They've been picking up
passengers all through the suburbs in the inner west.
So if you cannot stomach standing up and hanging
by the strap, smelling other people's sweaty misery
for fifteen minutes, take a bus that only goes to
Town Hall or the Queen Victoria Building. Those
buses often have more room. You'll see the sign on
the front of the bus.

Where are you from? You look like someone
I used to know, back when I might have given
directions by squatting down and drawing you a
mud map. But there's no mud here—nothing but
concrete as far as you can see.

If you *do* get off the bus at Town Hall or the
Queen Victoria Building, you can venture down
the tiled steps and into the sooty labyrinth of Town
Hall Station to try getting on a train, against the
flow. The suits will come at you, out of the train
and up the stairs. They will be a mindless mass of
charcoal grey and navy blue. They'll knock you over

if you don't push back, so be prepared to stand your ground. It nearly killed me when I got here, that wave of grim-faced workers.

Here's a tip, if you're not your best. The train to North Sydney is always emptier out of Wynyard and you can get on without a fight. So if you feel sad or out of sorts, don't get on at Town Hall. Just walk the three or four city blocks to Wynyard Station. If you feel sad or out of sorts, Town Hall could be the end of you.

If you do walk to Wynyard from Town Hall, keep to the left-hand side of the footpath. Don't meet anyone's eye and no-one will bump into you. If you look at them they walk right at you, as though they think you'll step aside.

Look down, not up. Upwards makes you look like you just came down from Coonabarabran, a wheat stalk in your mouth and lanolin in the creases of your hands. Don't smile too much. And never wave. Or even nod. You never saw these people before, these people you see each weekday morning.

And no matter where you catch the train, stay in the vestibule so you can look out the windows as you cross the Sydney Harbour Bridge and drink in the blueness of the water if it's blue. Or the sadness of the water if it's grey. The bridge can make a difference to your day. It will make you think, for just a minute, that all this crowded frantic pushing is worth the price you pay.

After you've crossed the bridge, it's Milson's Point station and as the train pulls out, get ready. There are others on the train who think it matters to be first. Just before North Sydney, they will push past you to stand as close as they can to the doors. They all want to be the first off the train, up the stairs and out the barriers. Get ready to be fierce. Protect your space or get out of the way.

Step out of the train. Shuffle forward with the mob. Follow them up the stairs and into Greenwood Plaza or out onto the street. Try not to think of sheep dogs and woolsheds. Stare straight ahead and step aside for the ones on urgent business.

Try and remember. Try and remember what brought you to Sydney. Why you thought this place would be better than the farm.

M

Belinda McCormick

I had this deal with a guy who owned a noodle joint. Sundays and Wednesdays I sucked his cock; he fed me and Gus. It was solid. Meant I didn't have to beg all day, scrounge slops half the night just to get by.

He caught us one night trawling for scraps in the alley out back of his shop. I pulled my head out of a bin and found Kung Fu fucking Panda leaning against a hopper, blocking our path.

I tried scoping a way past. I'm quick, but that alley was tighter than a Suit's wallet. No way I'd get by.

Top lip twitching, Gus slunk forward, dropped

to his belly. He had this way of sifting people, sorting the rotten.

Watched him go a guy once.

Behind a block of commission flats, we spotted this whack job. He had a fox strung up with barbed wire. Was so busy getting off on its struggles, Gus was ripping chunks off his arse before he even clocked us coming. Gave me a full-on laughing fit, but we were too late for Foxy. Dumb shit cut its own throat.

If Gus finds you whiffy, you'd best leg it early.

Noodle Boy just leaned and watched. When Gus rolled his weight onto one hip, the guy smiled so hard his cheeks swallowed his eyes.

'Hungry?' he said.

Last time we ate proper we'd lucked across a dero nursing half a leg of donated ham. Guts were so gone he couldn't hardly eat. Gave most of it to us. For two whole days my stomach didn't feel like it was eating itself.

Course we were hungry. We were always fucking hungry.

One wave of a meaty hand and Gus got up to follow.

At the back door Noodles told us to wait. Fine by me. Gus or no Gus, I wasn't going inside. Too easy to get done over. Besides, cold metal benches, sparkling white tiles. We'd have made it filthy.

Coupla minutes later, he came back with leftovers. Seeing as how I shared everything with Gus, it wasn't long before we were scoffing down seconds.

While we gutsed ourselves I thought about the guy's eyes. How shiny they went when he first looked me over.

A price was coming but he waited till we finished before naming it.

'You lick it,' he said, rubbing his crotch, 'I'll feed you again.'

If he'd tried anything else I'd have skipped out right then, not gone back.

Maybe he knew it, maybe not. Didn't stop us leaving. Just stepped aside, waved us off. 'Three days,' he said.

He was back inside locking up before we were out the gate.

Buggered if I'd let him find out where we slept. I cut across the street, turned the next corner, doubled back.

No sign of him following but a bunch of hoodies were coming up the block—the kind that might take a bat to you just for fun. Best not to hang around.

On the way back to our doss, I thought about the offer. Wasn't overly hot on it but I'd had worse things done to me on the off-chance of food.

Walked myself straight into a setup once.

I'd been out begging, pretending me and an older guy were family. People dropped dosh into our bucket like we were a church collection service. Was pretty sweet until the bastard sold me out.

Took me down the river. Said he'd found the perfect scam. Under a bridge, he pinned my arms, held me down while some skinny prick raped me.

Later, shovelling hot peas and mash, he called me a dumb shit. Said it was time I pulled my weight.

I bled for three days. Swore I'd never go back, never trust again.

A week later I found Gus lying in the gutter. Someone had tried to dock his tail. Wound was mostly healed, but he got dumped anyway.

We've been together ever since.

Watching Gus twitch in his sleep, tripping on a full belly, I thought about that promise. Wondered how far I was willing to stretch it.

By the end of the third day I had my answer. Leavings had been hard to come by. Told myself I owed it to Gus.

Hunger does that. Makes you twist things.

Anyone who tells you different hasn't ever had to think with their stomach.

We waited by the hoppers where we'd first seen the guy. Gus heard him coming. Stepped straight up to meet him, tail wagging so fast his arse went with it.

Noodles seemed as surprised as me. He bent down, scratched Gus behind the ears. I'd never seen anyone else do that.

This time we went to a room tacked onto one side out the back. Guy said it was his office. Left me to look it over while he finished cleaning up.

Wasn't much in there. A desk and chair with peeling vinyl. Wonky bookshelves full of dusty ring binders. A heavy combination safe.

Came back with a bag of bones. Just little ones but still with a fair amount of red on. Gus went all moon-eyed and slobbery. Looked full derpy on a Staffy.

A bucket of water and soap were next. Jesus. Couldn't remember the last time I'd touched real soap. Noodles set them down on my side of the desk, moved around to the chair.

If I was gonna bail, now was the time.

I watched him watching me. 'Your choice,' he said.

Wasn't real keen about being inside till he told me I could leave the door open.

Hadn't really known what to expect but was pretty sure this wasn't it. Even the wet-dog stink of the carpet made it feel like home.

Maybe it did to him too.

I washed my hands, my face, my neck. I'd have done my hair too but I didn't want to risk pissing him off. Pushing the bucket aside, I looked him in the eye.

'Done this before?' he asked.

I shook my head. Hoped it went in my favour.

'Okay,' he said, undoing his fly. 'Give me your hand.'

Didn't take long to show me what he liked. Talked the whole time about pressure, speed, tongue versus thumb, mouth versus hand. It was over quicker than I expected.

After, he pulled a framed photo out of the desk drawer. Stared at it creepish long before asking my name.

I told him 'M'. Decided I liked it.

'Em? Like for Emma?'

He thought I was a girl. Sometimes that's a good thing. Girls get more handouts. They're also easier targets. I'm young and skinny enough to pass for either so long as you don't go feeling me up.

When I didn't answer, he shrugged. 'I'll call you Empty,' he said. 'Em for Empty.'

I've called him Fool ever since, but I wasn't daft enough to say it out loud. When you find someone willing to feed you, you don't hand them a reason to stop. Not even when things start smelling ripe.

Before last night he never seemed to care if I swallowed or spat. He never hurt me either. Hardly touched me at all. This time was different.

Soon as I went to work on him, he started yabbering at me. He always was a great talker— during. But this was something else. Didn't sound like instructions. Wasn't even sure it was English.

Arms waving, gut heaving, it was all I could do to stay with him. Was thinking about stopping when he grabbed the back of my head, pulled me forward. I realised then that he was crying. Even as I struggled not to choke, the crying bothered me more than anything. Maybe Gus too—I could hear him whining outside on the porch.

When Fool was done I didn't want to look at him. He kept snuffling, wiping at his nose while he groped for the bag of food. He set it down and reached for a second bag. Inside were an overcoat and a pair of too-bright Nikes.

Presents? I tried not to think about what that might mean.

I pulled out the coat. Black. Heavy wool. Warmer than everything else I owned put together. If I stayed low a few days it'd reek of gutter leavings and foot-rot. Enough to blend in, go unnoticed. But those shoes were gonna be trouble.

Wouldn't be bagging any freebies. Not wearing a month's food money on my feet. Wasn't stupid enough to try selling them either. Fastest way to a bad end, that one.

Maybe I could keep the coat, leave the shoes.

Fool wouldn't take no for an answer. He shoved the bag at me, gestured at my worn-out boots. Soon as I had them off, he threw them in the hopper. Didn't mind that so much. Garbage wouldn't be collected for almost a week. I'd be back to get them before then.

He hung around like always, watching us eat. I got to thinking maybe things might go back to normal. Not happening. Instead of leaving us to it when we finished eating, this time he stayed. Even followed us out the alley when we left. Didn't say a word, but I felt the weight of his gaze track me up the street.

A block further on it started to rain. Heavy

drops pelted my face. Some part of me wanted to stand there, let the water wash everything away.

Gus was having none of it. He took off down the street. I wasn't surprised. He knew better than me where to find shelter.

Part way along, he pulled up short, ducked down a narrow lane. He'd seen what I hadn't. Five or six hoods taking shelter in a bus stop. They might have missed him but my feet were like glow-worms. One guy stood up, shouted.

I went after Gus, picked up his lead. Backstreets round here were a maze of switchbacks. We'd be gone, so long as we made the first coupla corners. Rain thrumming off the awnings, I didn't think they'd chase for long.

Turned out they didn't have to.

Gus skidded full-pelt round a corner, straight into a junkie cutting lines. White powder punched out into the open, fell back to the ground as rain. Only score he'd likely find on a night turned sour, gone.

Gangs are bad if you get caught, but they're not that hard to avoid. Addicts are something else.

Angry red splotches covered this one's face. He was riding pretty close to the edge.

I held out my hands, tried backing away.

Two steps and he had me hard against a wall, hands fisted together in the front of my coat. He lifted a knee, caught me in the gut.

My breath woofed out, doubled me over. A second knee up under my chin snapped my head back into the wall. My knees crumpled, I went down.

Gus loomed up out of the dark, latched onto my attacker's arm. It was never gonna be enough.

A dull blade glinted murder in the night. Red ran thin in the downpour. Once, twice, three times. Greyness grew around me and I lost count. By then it didn't matter. Gus lay as still as me.

The sound of his whimpers drew me back. I'd been hearing them for some time. Soft and forlorn, like the puppy noises he made the night we met. They tugged at me now like they had then, dragging me back to myself.

Don't know how long we lay there, together but apart. It was the apartness I couldn't stand. Shoes were gone and I hurt all over but far as I could tell I wasn't cut. I pushed myself up, crawled to Gus. All the while his stump of a tail thumped the cold asphalt.

Just as I reached him the rain stopped. Pink froth bubbled from his nose. A pool too thick to wash away lay dark beneath his gut. I draped an arm across his shoulders, drew my body up around his. He relaxed into me, whimpers calming as he began to drift.

He passed sometime before dawn.

Next day I held onto him. Watched that scene play out on an endless loop. Tried to change it in my head, give it a happy ending. I couldn't do it. Kept coming back to those fucking shoes.

After dark I duffled Gus in my coat, carried him across my shoulders. Wearing threadbare socks not yet grown into my skin, I went back to see Fool.

If I'd gone up the alley I'd have seen it straight away. But I'd come down the street, right to the front door. I wanted to be seen struggling under the weight. Wanted people to wonder why I was there.

Safety tape blocked the front of the building but I didn't want to believe. I'd been smelling it of course. Wet ash, burnt wood. Claggy but sharp, it hung over the whole block.

I hoisted Gus one more time, trudged around to the alley.

The entire back half of the building was gone. Charred beams lay open to the sky. Clumps of twisted metal, glass and tile stood out against the grey.

There's no way Fool died in the fire. The way the bastard acted, I reckon he did a runner. I hated him for that, but I hated myself more.

I'd gone there wanting to lay Gus at Fool's feet, watch his face when he saw what he'd done. I'd thought maybe then I'd know what to do. But if I hadn't got so fucking used to things, I'd have seen it all coming, taken steps. Gus would still be alive.

As it was, I placed his body atop a mound of ashes, draped my new coat around him. I thought about putting him inside the building, but I wanted him to be found. Even if I was the only person who understood why he was there.

I checked the hopper. Boots were right where they landed. I put them on, went to look at the office. Safe was still there. I sat on it, tried to make sense of things. My gaze wandered till I spied the corner of a silver frame poking out of the rubble.

Most of the woman's head remained undamaged. Below her shoulder one side of the photo had blistered. But you could tell she was wearing a wedding dress.

The fall of her hair, the line of her neck, even the cast of her eyes. I didn't need a fucking mirror. Any younger and she'd have passed for me.

All the Places You Have Been

Erin Courtney Kelly

Clare and her daughter are waiting in line to see the rotting body of a corpse flower. All her daughter is interested in is the promise of an ice-cream once they filter through the glasshouse, slowly push through the humidity and the stench of something dying, and see the already-dead flower.

Clare pushes against the feeling of nausea and panic and tries to look at her daughter the way the other mums do. She looks at Olive's small fingers and the way her legs seem stiff when she walks, a baby giraffe still learning, she looks at her hair and the way it is too shiny, like plastic, to be real.

They are still in the line when the sun turns

on them; Clare feels her skin shrinking as it burns. Olive is still in the shade, too small for the sun to reach yet. Clare pulls her hand out of Olive's and pulls her ponytail off her shoulders, wanting the skin on both of her shoulders to match in pinkness. Hopefully they will be inside the hothouse by the time the sun reaches Olive; Clare didn't bring any sunscreen.

The people in the queue are getting restless as the sun moves lower on their shoulders. Clare feels a drop of sweat roll down from her armpit and onto the waistband of her underpants. Olive stands patiently, watching the magpies peck at the grass, and Clare watches the woman in front of her, an older woman whose skin hangs loose and cool around her. The woman seems to wear her skin like she is happy. Clare feels the prickle of her own skin; doubt licks her arms and releases a ripple of goose bumps. She wonders whether she should be here and then she remembers that her questions always get her into trouble.

The most damaging of the questions was the one she had asked so long ago, why is he looking at me like that? The next one was even more complicated and she still wasn't certain that she had made the right choice. She had had to bury that question though, deep into the shadow of her growing belly so that her body could not feel it burning her anymore. She had been surprised to find herself giving birth, that she had decided to keep it after all.

When she eventually told the father, he was pleased, happy even, and insisted on flying out right away. She had looked at Olive after getting off the phone with him and imagined that Olive had already picked sides and it wasn't hers.

With her skin seizing around her as they wait for the chance to see the dying flower, Clare knows she's not here for Olive; she doesn't care that Olive might hate the flower, might cry at the smell, she knows that she is just here for herself.

The line starts moving slowly and Olive takes uncertain steps, pulling down on Clare's arm. It seems strange but necessary that she is waiting with her daughter to see a flower die as soon as it blooms. She needs to be reminded of how fast everything can still change.

She was waiting in line at the pub. It was a Sunday afternoon and the inside of the pub was dark and smelt like stale beer but people still drank fast. Clare was thinking of her drinks order, Sav for Stel, pint for her and Mim, when she smelt something like pine needles and the heady smell of a forest floor. She turned around and the man behind her smiled. She smiled and smelt the faraway smell of pine forests. She turned back to the bar. She got to the front of the queue. He was still behind her, she could smell him and the smell clawed at her skin, made her homesick.

It was a smell that was so far away from London. London smelt like pollution, rain on dirty roads and curry; it smelt like a city that crushed all the delicate smells into dirt.

Clare remembered the days when she would drive out to the Dandenong ranges and run through the bush. Her lungs would haul the clean air in as fast as she could make them. The bush would be dripping with rain, ferns flicking dots of water at her cheeks and every footstep released the smell of pine needles and thick, moist soil.

She picked up the glasses, turned and he almost fell into the three drinks held precariously in her fingers. His face was close to hers, his hair smelt like the forest. Stel and Mim would laugh when she told them that for a moment she thought he was the forest come to take her away.

Stel and Mim looked up at her as she placed the drinks in front of them on the table.

'What's that look on your face for then?' Mim asked, never one to miss something as fleeting as an expression of possibility.

'Nothing,' Clare said, the look still clearly drawn all over her face.

'Come on,' Stel said, her red lips pressed onto the rim of her wine glass.

'You guys will laugh.'

'Yeah, we probably will.'

'Just tell us anyway,' Stel pushed her glasses further up her nose as if this was the cue for Clare to start talking.

'There was a guy at the bar, he smelt like the forest.'

They laughed and Clare shook her head, she shouldn't have said anything. They would never let her hear the end of it.

'The forest, that's new,' Mim said, her long black hair almost dipping into her pint glass as she threw her head forward with laughter.

'I like it, it's romantic,' Stel said, her eyes darting around the pub searching for a man who looked like he could smell like the forest.

'It was just unexpected, that's all.' Clare slurped the froth off the top of her pint.

Stel and Mim were eager for Clare to find

someone, to bury her life deep into someone else as they had done, but Clare had always resisted settling down. She had stopped talking about men she was interested in with her friends because usually they talked the relationship to death before it had even started. Clare would feel she had already lived a whole life with the person before the second date, and she always saw how it ended, with her bored and running away.

She focused instead on retreading the memories from their younger days when they worked in pubs, had no money and lived like white-hot flames, volatile and fast.

Clare watched the expressions rapidly change on people's faces around her, anxious, bored, exhausted, no-one was happy to be at the start of their journey.

The queue was long, wriggling, and bloated where families huddled together as they all waited to board.

Her stomach was already floating away with nerves, anxious to know what she would find at the other end. Would they see each other and feel happy or would they look at each other through the sides of their eyes and wonder what had brought them to this station in France after one night together?

They had held hands sitting on stools in the pub. They had held hands all the way home through the rain to her house; they had held hands like they wanted to experience everything together, like they could see the world the same way, from the same brain, if they held on to each other. It had felt like they wanted to see everything as much as they could through their one existence. She felt like that feeling had no ending; from that night it would just go on forever.

The romance of that night had crushed them both like they were petals; it had bruised them with the speed of it.

At the pub Stel and Mim had talked Clare into going back over to the man with the forest beard and asking him how it was that his beard smelt so good.

He whispered that he liked to go into forests and rub his beard against the trees. She had laughed and he had caught her eyes in his.

He had seemed flattered that she had laughed at his terrible joke and she slid easily onto the wooden stool next to him asking him how someone from deep in the forest came to be in a pub in London. He had pointed to the man in a suit across the other side of the pub.

'He's the lucky groom to be.'

She laughed and asked, 'Where are you from? You have a very confusing accent.'

'I live in France but was born here. You have a very Australian accent.'

'They're harder to hide than British accents.'

It was his turn to laugh and her turn to blush at the way his eyes broke into hers.

For the next few hours they sat side by side at the bar, his arms crossed on the bar top and his body leaning over them, her drink held back in her lap. Their friends would pop in and out of conversation but the flickering of her stomach made her want to know if what she was feeling was the same as him. She reached up to put her glass on the bar and he took the glass from her and then took her hand. She felt the sweat suddenly sting in her palms but he wouldn't let go and they sat hand in hand as the pub started to empty. Stel and Mim kissed her on the cheek goodbye in a blur of lipstick and smiles.

Outside on a street wet with rain he took her hand again and wrapped it around his back, pulling her into his body and she didn't have time to swallow her nerves before he was kissing her, her hands reached up to his chin, the softness of his beard surprised her.

203

Now, in the queue at the station she wondered if it was real, if that had been a true feeling.

She looked at the faces close to her, lingered on their expressions, tried to learn from what they were telling her. People were trying to look like they were being patient but the darting of their eyes betrayed them. People were watching for the train as if it would bring a cure for their loneliness. Clare waited for the train with a look on her face like she had no idea what was coming for her.

The place that bulk-billed was always packed and Clare had turned up early, not to beat the queue so much, more to know for sure so that she didn't have to feel this dread any longer; it was making her sick.

The day outside was already oppressive in that way that a summer in Melbourne sometimes was, heavy heat pressing on the city for days with nowhere for it to go.

She had flown home with nausea nipping at her the whole way and she wasn't sure whether she felt terrible because of how she had skipped out the door and left him behind or if she was actually just terrified of coming back to her hometown.

She had slipped out before he could talk her out of it. She had wondered if what was happening between them was imaginary, if her brain had filled in the gaps of what she wanted and when she looked at it front on it actually wasn't real.

Clare had gone to the pub before she left to talk it over with Stel and Mim. Stel said to stick with it and Mim just told her to fuck him off if he wasn't what she wanted. The angel and the devil were always there for her, looking out for her in different ways.

She hadn't known she was pregnant then and she was drinking beer like she wanted a hangover that would hurt her. Then both Stel and Mim started looking at her like she needed taking care of and Clare knew that something in her wasn't right.

'So, what was it again, that made you leave?' Stel asked, hoping that if Clare said it one more time that she would realise what an idiot she was being and go back to the man who they all liked for his kind nature and beard that smelt like the forest.

'I told you, it wasn't anything he did so much as what I could see happening in the future.'

'Fuck him before he fucks you,' Mim said definitively.

'But you can't see the future, how do you know what would happen?' Stel quickly jumped in.

Clare gulped her beer and tried.

'There he was at the train station and he loved me already, it was on his face before I even arrived.'

'Jesus, sounds awful,' Mim rolled her eyes.

'It wasn't real. It was an imagined woman he was waiting for. He was like that before he saw me. He didn't look at me like that when he finally saw me.'

Stel slapped her glass on the wet table. 'He loved you! What more did you want from him?'

'I kept having to look at the world for the two of us and that was exhausting. I wanted to be able to be separate from him.'

Clare felt exhausted talking through it again. Stel and Mim peered at her carefully.

'Don't worry, love, we got you.' Mim patted Clare's hand and pushed Clare's pint glass closer to her.

They sat in silence as their bodies sweated onto the leather of the pub booth. The heaters were up high to combat the slush of winter that tried to break into the pub every time the door opened.

They wouldn't go back to that pub again; the three of them were flung to other sides of the world shortly after that. Clare back to Australia with a growing body inside her, Stel to her relatives in Lithuania to care for a dying grandparent and Mim

to Fiji for work, where they often lost contact with
her as the storm season drifted over and knocked her
Internet out.

Clare sat on the edge of the sandpit and waited with
the rest of the parents who were arranged around
the playground in some kind of ugly afternoon
tableau of tired faces and tracksuit pants. The bell
rang and Clare heard the scramble of kids from
inside the building. She kept her eyes on the door
that Olive would tumble out of, too young to stop
her body from propelling itself into the other kids
as they came out the door. Olive had started going
for full days at school and when she came out she
was so full of stories that she would talk all the way
through dinner and right up until Clare put the light
out. It was these parts of parenting that made Clare
feel more like a vessel and not a real human being.
She had no stories to tell Olive, cleaning the house
or shopping for food was not a story.

Olive's dad would be over again soon, taking
care of Olive for a month or two, and then Clare
could go and create some stories for herself. She
had no plans apart from, get out of town and forget
the little face and the father who loved his daughter
with such clarity that Clare wondered if he was

made of anything but pure emotions. She felt like
a serrated blade, destructive. Clare had worked
out too late that her feelings about having a kid
were complicated and she wasn't allowed to take a
way out. She kept her eyes on the door, imagining
the kids scrambling to their bags, pushing in their
schoolbooks, already gathering the stories ready to
blurt at their parents.

There was a woman smoking next to Clare,
occasionally the smoke would drift over and burn
Clare's nostrils open. She eventually stopped and
ground the butt into the playground dirt. She sat
next to Clare on the edge of the sandpit. Clare
looked at the woman's arms, clutched around her
knees; they were like aged leather, stretched, tough.

'I was listening to the radio on the way over here
and I heard this story about a dead flower.'

The woman didn't bother with an introduction,
it didn't matter who she was, they were all just
anonymous parents.

'Apparently it just blooms and then dies. Just
like that. In, like, a weekend. Bizarre.'

Clare grunted with interest, her eyes scanning
the faces of the kids now bursting out of the door.

'It's in the Gardens at the moment but it'll be
dead by Sunday.'

Clare barely heard the last sentence; she had seen Olive's face through the blur of the other school kids running towards the playground.

Olive came running up, half a sentence already out of her mouth. She stormed through the stories so fast that Clare could only manage a brief smile in the direction of the other woman, who was also now tangled in the limbs of her child.

It wasn't until Olive was in bed that Clare had time to catch up with the story the woman had told her earlier that day.

She typed the name into her computer and the images that appeared on the screen were of a huge purple skirt, pleated around a two-metre yellow stamen. Scrolling further down, the pictures were of the flaccid collapse of the flower, the rotting flesh lolling like a purple tongue, wasted.

She knew that the flower was something that she wanted to see in front of her. To look at how this would have ended. To imagine the brief spectacle she could have lived, to imagine that she had never grown up.

Still Life with Dying Swan

Gail Chrisfield

The bathhouse change cubicle is half the size of my en suite. Its oppressive walls are the same bland lemon chiffon. The faux marble floor tiles almost match our genuine ones. If I felt better, its clinical seclusion might appeal less. The previous occupant's lingering Lily of the Valley perfume brings on a sneeze that threatens to blow my head off.

Someone taps on the door. 'You okay in there?' The familiar voice cuts through the muffled change area noises outside.

'Yep. I'll be out in a minute,' I say, wiping my nose with the back of my hand.

'I'm here if you need me.'

'Okey-dokey.'

Poking my tongue out at my daughter on the other side, I peel both thighs off the lacquered timber seat and re-read the notice taped to the door. The words still make no sense so I poke my tongue at them too and shift my attention to my wasted body.

Beneath the stark, fluorescent light, my skin is bleached of all colour, aside from the blue veins snaking up each calf and the red marks tracking down both forearms. The colostomy bag pinches inside my baggy swimsuit. A snug fit on its last outing.

'Mum, other people are waiting.'

'Coming.'

I take my time wrapping and tying the white bathrobe. Ali was the one who wanted to come here. 'It will be so good for you, Mum.' How often has she said that over the past six months?

'She's only trying to help,' I repeat under my breath before unlocking the door.

A handful of self-absorbed bathers are immersed in the relaxation pool's aquamarine hues and soothing mood music. Ali laughs. 'Don't look so shocked, Mum. Didn't I tell you there'd hardly be anyone here?'

She helps me out of my robe and guides me to the ramp. No-one laughs at my awkward gait. Unlike the two of us earlier, giggling at a clumsy swan, waddling behind the more fleet-footed ducks and geese competing for Ali's prize of a few scattered bread crusts.

I grip the handrail, flinching at the cold steel against my palm, and wade through ankle-deep water to navigate the steps. I let go and sink into balmy syrup from shoulders to toes. My body sighs as minerals seep through skin and muscles, and the pain leaches from my bones.

I tiptoe to the window. The water supports my arms as if I am a bird hovering over a thermal. My feet lift and settle wherever its gentle oscillation takes them. The left deviates too far and I lose balance, almost colliding with a woman in a purple bathing cap. I return her blissed-out smile as we pass, en route to opposite ends.

The window frames the still landscape outside. In the fading light, the treetops are burnished by late afternoon sun, their trunks tarnished by shadow. A swirling mass of white against green breaks the spell. Cockatoos on their way home before nightfall.

Folding my arms to bolster my head, I close my eyes and breathe deeply. My legs rise and fall with each breath in and out. Their buoyancy gives me a sense of how it might feel to be an astronaut floating in space.

Cold air brushes the nape of my neck, bringing me back to earth. When I turn, Ali's watching, a smile playing on her face. I dog paddle across the pool to join her on the underwater couch.

'Is that Japanese flute music?' I ask.

'Uh-huh.' She leans back and closes her eyes. 'Shakuhachi.'

'It's lovely—so calming.'

'Uh-huh. Very Zen.'

We loll in companionable silence until the light catches my knees below the water.

'What's so funny, Mum?'

'My knees look like Whatshername on that stupid show you and Matt used to watch with your father every Saturday night.'

Ali opens her eyes and chuckles. 'Mrs McGillicuddy.'

'That's it. Mrs McGillicuddy. Ms Alison Payne, may I introduce you to Mrs McGillicuddy and her husband, Mr McGillicuddy.'

We laugh as if my prune-faced knees are the

funniest things we've ever seen. 'Shush,' a passing bather says, reminding us we're not alone.

'It's good to hear you laugh again, Mum.' Ali's eyes glisten. She eases off the couch and walks towards the spa end of the pool.

Lounging against the tiles, I close my eyes so my thoughts can roam wherever they want. They take me back home to the start of everything changing. The long nights I spent lying awake in the dark, panicking about what was going to happen.

One night I realised everyone talks about only living once. But you only die once too. I decided I wanted a good death, a quiet slipping away. Most nights since, I've slept well.

Before my diagnosis, a rushed weekly phone call was often the best Ali could manage to fit me in to her busy schedule. Career, fitness and social life took up all her time. Now I do.

'Mum, I'll do whatever I can to help you beat this thing,' she told me in the hospital, between fussing with the flowers and cards. I asked her to leave them but she likes to be in charge of things.

This morning, we argued about the massage she'd booked for me. It might have helped during the first few months of swinging between denial and anger. Another stranger's hands on my body at this stage would be more awkward than relaxing.

Ali refused to concede and the pretty, young masseuse backed her up. 'Your treatment,' she kept repeating, oblivious about the meaning of that word to a cancer patient.

In the end, I kept the peace by agreeing to a private aromatherapy bath. It was pleasant enough. I prefer it here though, among other anonymous public bathers. It beats staring at the wall, counting down the lonely minutes.

The Japanese flutes end, replaced by the pool's tranquil symphony of gurgling water. It's too dark outside to see the trees.

I slide from the couch, touch down and tiptoe forward, studying the whorls each step creates on the pool floor. Their fusions and fissions remind me of cells under a microscope.

I lift my feet and glide above them, a graceful swan swimming on the lake. I can't remember the last time life felt this good.

And then Ali says, 'It's too quiet. Can you put the music back on? Please.'

I swallow a mouthful of water and go under. I resurface, coughing, and regain my footing.

Everyone's watching Ali. The uniformed attendant kneels on the pool deck and says something only she can hear.

'Well, turn it up then,' she demands.

Before I can apologise for her rude behaviour, he's walking away shaking his head. The other bathers resume their vacuous gazes and languid movements.

'Are you okay, sweetie?'

'I can't hear the music.' Ali's face is a picture of childish petulance. 'Can you?'

She slaps the water. Its ripples burble over the tiles. The sound bounces off the windows and walls, harmonising with my mood.

'It's not funny, Mum. Why are you laughing?'

'Seriously, sweetie, does it really matter?'

'Yes. It matters a lot. I just want everything to be perfect.'

She smacks the water again and turns to get out of the pool.

The door slides open and I follow Ali outside. The chill sets in before I can zip up my jacket.

'Ali,' I moan, jamming my hands into the pockets and pulling the padded fabric tighter. It does nothing to stop the shivering. The pain returns, radiating from the base of my spine, down my legs and up into my chest and shoulders.

'Here, Mum.' She slides one arm around my back, drawing me against her. I clutch her free hand, feeling her wince in the dark.

We inch our way across the bridge to the car park. Each step is like walking on broken glass. Ali tells me to keep going, I'm doing well and we're almost there. She says it again and again, until I've had enough.

'Cut the crap.' My hips seize and I stop, pulling her back with a strength that surprises us both.

'It's not much further, Mum. We're almost there.'

'God, I hate it when you lie to me, Ali.' She says nothing. I try to hold back. The tears keep coming. 'I can't do this anymore.'

'It's okay, Mum.' Ali props me against the railing and hands over a wad of tissues. 'Wait here. I'll get the car. Be back in a minute.'

Her hasty footsteps crunch on the gravel path and fade away. I hope this time she's telling the truth.

In the early morning light, the lake's unruffled surface offsets the chaos on the foreshore. Two yapping dogs, a crying swan and a woman screaming, 'Here! Here! Come here!'

Ali joins me at the kitchen window. 'What's going on down there?' she asks, rubbing the sleep from her eyes.

The swan rears and flaps her wings. Her long neck writhes and her red beak snaps. The dogs are too quick. As she tries to fend off one, the other moves in to attack her exposed breast. She twists his way, leaving her back unprotected against his partner's savagery. Black feathers swirl in the breeze and drift to the ground.

The laundry door slams and, a moment later, Ali is sprinting down the hill. She plants her feet and throws out her arms. 'Get away, you mongrels!'

The dogs recoil. The woman leaps forward and grabs one by the collar. Ali nabs the other and yanks it away. My eyes tear up with pride. She's been afraid of dogs since childhood. She doesn't let this one go until it's leashed.

The woman shakes her head and stamps her feet. Straining to return to their quarry, neither dog takes any notice. Ali holds both leads while the woman makes a phone call. The swan lies broken on the ground.

The woman walks out of view, dragging the

dogs behind her. Ali squats beside the swan and fondles the disheveled wings wrapped around the arched back. The swan stretches her neck and lifts her head for a heartbeat.

Ali's back heaves and her shoulders shudder. I haven't seen my daughter cry since her ex dumped her. Her grief broke my heart. Witnessing her breakdown now, after she's held it together for so long, brings a strange relief.

Two men appear, one carrying blankets, the other a case. Ali moves away, blowing her nose on her dressing gown. They finish examining the swan, lay out a blanket and slide her into the middle. Lifting each end, they carry the makeshift stretcher up the hill and out of sight. Ali follows with their gear.

I'm sitting back at the table when she returns. 'Is the swan going to be okay, sweetie?'

'No,' she says in between sobs. 'They have to put it down.'

As our car pulls into the driveway, Mick is waiting on the porch. He springs down the stairs two at a time, meeting Ali at the bottom. She disappears inside his fatherly bear hug for several moments, reappears and heads inside.

Mick grins through the windscreen and opens my door. 'I'm so glad you're home, darling. I missed you.'

'It was only for one night.'

We both laugh as he helps untangle my seatbelt and takes me in his arms. His well-worn jumper tickles my face. I nuzzle into its thick wool, imbued with his familiar aroma of Ralph Lauren tinged with wood smoke and whiskey. Inhaling deeply, I try to draw as much of it as I can to store inside for later.

'How did it go?'

'Fine, but I think it did Ali more good than me.'

'Sounds like it. When I spoke to her this morning, something had shifted.'

I reach up and pluck a dead leaf off his shoulder. 'It's time.'

Mick nods. 'I know. I've called Matt. His plane gets in at six.'

I'm floating amid the cosy scent of freshly washed, sun-kissed sheets. Matt squeezes my hand, anchoring me to my king-size bed. 'Love you to bits, Mum.'

'Love you … too.' I want to say more. My tongue has gone to sleep. A bitter, chemical taste lingers in my mouth.

'You're the love of my life, Annie. Always have been, always will be.' Mick rubs an ice chip over my parched lips.

I smile and the cold liquid trickles inside. It races down my tongue and stalls at the back of my throat until I swallow. Struggling to keep my eyes open, I drink in one last look at the faces around me.

Mick and Matt sit alongside, holding a hand each. Ali's reclining at the end of the bed, stroking my feet through the doona. When I close my eyes, the trio is imprinted on my eyelids.

'Ali, love, can you take over here for a minute?' Mick detaches his huge, warm hand and wriggles off the bed. He sniffles.

Matt releases my other hand and slides away. 'It's okay, Dad, you're allowed to cry. Isn't he, Mum?' I can't respond.

'You're the best, Mum,' Ali whispers.

She rubs my hand with a cool, delicate touch. Father and son are exchanging manly back pats. They haven't done that since Matt's wedding. Their voices were resonant with joy. Now they're strangled by tears.

Ali sighs beside me. 'I've tried to stop all this from happening but I can't. It's time to let you go, Mum. I will never stop loving you, I will never stop missing you and I will never stop trying to be the best I can—for you and our funny little family.'

Her wet cheek brushes against mine. She holds it there, drenching my face with her tears. If I could, I'd wrap my arms around her and give her one last hug.

'You okay, sis?' Matt settles on the bed and takes my other hand.

Her face leaves mine. 'I'm fine, thanks.'

'Why don't I make us a nice cup of tea?' Mick asks.

'Not just now, Dad,' my children reply in unison. 'Snap.'

While they're laughing, I allow myself to sink back into the soothing warm syrup. Its gentle current carries me towards the swan. Together, we quietly slip away.

Joiner Bay

Laura Elvery

I'm a runner. I don't get pocket money for jobs or just because. Dad tells everyone how if I run ten ks he'll give me five bucks. If I get a PB I get five dollars more. We have the rowing machine and the weights and a bench press in the spare room now. I've been running more lately, and someone else, like a psychologist, might say it's because my best friend died recently. But people can say what they like, and they still won't know the truth, even if they believe it. Even if they tell other adults while I'm in the room. My best friend's name was Robbie. You don't need to know his last name, because nobody cares about that. But what you will care about is that he killed himself, and you'll care how he did it: with a cord and a beam to hang from, which means he probably broke his neck, and then he probably stopped breathing. That's the order of things.

Last night I set my alarm for four-thirty. When it goes off, I get up and take a piss without turning the light on. I get dressed and have a sip of water, only a sip, so I don't get a stitch. I used to listen to music with my headphones but one night I was almost hit by a car—my fault—driven by the school librarian. Our town, Lusk, is pretty small, and Mr Rigby didn't seem annoyed that he'd almost been in an accident with a student. He didn't yell. He motioned me over to say that I had three library books overdue and they'd soon start attracting a fine. I liked him a lot after that. I found the books in my room and went to school to hand them over and he said, 'What? Put them in the chute.'

After Robbie died, Mr Rigby never tried talking to me about suicide and I liked him even more after that.

So to be able to hear the traffic, I ditched the headphones and now I have to listen to my thoughts.

I'm going to run ten ks and show Dad my Strava when I get home so he'll give me five bucks after breakfast. I'll run my usual route into town, past the

murals along Dartmouth Street and out to Joiner
Bay where they want to build a big coal port that
might kill everything in the reef. Not much we can
do about that, Dad says, and I agree. It'll be tied
up for years, anyway, and there's a lot to be said
for seeing how things pan out, and not getting too
worried about small things we can't change.

So now you know I like running and that I had
a best friend called Robbie and that the only way to
make any money in my house where I live with my
dad and the bench press and a bedroom where there
are sometimes overdue library books is to rack up
the ks on a big loop out to the hill above Joiner Bay.

I run out of our driveway and along our wide,
dead-quiet street towards the murals that Lusk is
famous for. The first is of a horse and carriage, and
next to that is the mural of the train driving towards
you, but the perspective is all off so it tugs at your
guts and makes you feel sick. The Lusk family
who founded our town are painted in the next one
against the back wall of the church. Stuart Lusk and
his three sons are sharp and mean in an oval frame
like a brooch. The smallest son looks like a total
murderer, as though he killed a family up in the hills
and then wiped his hands and sat down to dinner
with his dad and brothers. Without music to listen

to I have the same thoughts each time, and there's nothing I can do to come up with new ones.

I run. The sky lightens. The sun rises above Joiner Bay, which is shaped like an embrace, with two arms of rocky hills reaching into the water. The flowers on the trees are white and pink and yellow. There aren't many houses out here. Set back from the road is the caravan park with a post box and a telephone booth out the front, and a fibreglass pool with a waterslide that gets jammed with kids during summer.

After Robbie killed himself in our shed, Dad said, 'Isn't it strange, Jake, that he brought that cord with him?' Dad likes having a mate to talk to, and that's usually me, and he always says exactly what's on his mind.

I'd already thought about the cord. 'Maybe he didn't think we had one in there.'

'We don't,' Dad said.

'He must have known.'

At least one night a week Robbie came over to chat with Dad and me while we exercised. He wandered around, inspecting the equipment, cradling dumbbells. He knew we had a rowing machine and a bench press and a whole range of beams to choose from, painted dark green. Now,

when teachers at school talk about caring for each
other and about preventative measures, they're
not talking about having no beams, or no access
to cords. Every single person in Lusk has a theory
about why Robbie killed himself. Theories they've
hunkered down with and won't let go of. They've
all used their imaginations very hard, sipping
milkshakes in the café in town and sharing their
imaginations with someone else. They've locked
the front door at night and sat at the kitchen table,
bobbing a tea bag up and down in a thinking way.

I stop for water at the fountain and rinse it
through my mouth, spitting it onto the road. I still
haven't seen anybody on foot in town this morning,
only a few utes and delivery trucks. I pause the
Strava so my time is still good, and I think about
Robbie. He was short. He had bad breath. He liked
watching Formula One racing and soccer on TV.
He went to church. He had two younger sisters
he spoiled with those glittery kid magazines from
the supermarket. Robbie liked that I was nice to
the twins and he made me promise I'd help them
when they got to high school. The week before it all
happened, he followed me around the library at the
end of lunch, bored, slipping books out and putting
them back spine-in. He found a hardcover about

celebrities who died young and he kept on coming
back to the shelf to read it. He showed it to me. I
think I thought it was funny.

Lusk is hot. Even in May. Even at five a.m.
I press restart on my phone and spring from the
balls of my feet towards the hill that will take me
to the water. Years ago, Robbie and I sat on the
sand at Joiner Bay for pretty much the whole month
of January to watch a movie being filmed on the
peninsula. They'd built a pirate ship with sails and
cannons and a mermaid on the front. We ate fish
and chips and mucked around in the water. Robbie
reckoned we should swim out to spy on the actors,
but we never did.

And where was I when Robbie fished the spare
key from inside the drain pipe and entered the shed?
And where was Dad? We'd gone for a sunset run,
on our other usual route, in the opposite direction,
past the war memorial and out to Opal Bay. Dad
promised me ten dollars for a PB. We came home
through the front door, and I took off my sneakers
and T-shirt and Dad passed me a water bottle.
He did some high knee-jumps on the tiles. He
stretched out his hip flexors and tossed me the TV
remote from under the couch. I watched a bunch of
things—about how to catch black bream with river

prawns, about how much a three-hundred-year-old jade pendant is worth, about Olympic athletes who almost died when they took steroids in the eighties.

We ate dinner. I folded the ten-dollar note into the envelope in my desk drawer and went to bed. While I was asleep, Dad had gone out to the shed to use the rowing machine. He found Robbie and made the phone calls and stayed up all night. When I woke up, I saw Dad crouched beside my bed, wet from the shower. My muscles were tender after a dreamless sleep.

He said, 'Mate.'

My first thought was that he'd injured himself. Still sleepy, I leant over to check his legs.

'My little mate.'

Robbie was heavy, Dad had said. Heavy and peaceful. That last bit Dad made up, as if I didn't have the imagination to know what really might happen when your neck breaks and you suffocate in the grey light outside your best friend's house. Robbie's trouble was with his church, someone said. His trouble was with a new girl from school. A clutch of older boys. His trouble was with his father, always far-flung and gloomy, who seemed to rally himself better after Robbie's death than he ever had before.

On the footpath winding up the hill, I dodge

dozens of jackfruit that have split open. They are fat,
fluorescent, mammalian. I see and hear the ocean. I
try to steady my breath in through my nose and out
my mouth. The coal port out on the water is more
solid than a simple idea. It's an unshelved book,
harbouring secrets. What's to stop me right now
from running into the ocean? Endorphins, are what
Dad thinks. The shed is empty now and we don't go
in there but endorphins will protect us both.

I reach the halfway point at one of the outcrops
overlooking the bay. I press pause and reach for my
toes. My theory about what stopped Robbie from
doing it at his own house were his sisters: cross-
legged on the floor of the bedroom they shared,
peeling stickers from the magazines and placing
them like medallions down their legs. That's all I've
come up with—he didn't leave a note. Back at school
after the funeral, I checked the library shelves for
spine-in books, thinking maybe Robbie was into
clues and secrets, even though he'd never talked
about clues and secrets with me. I turned a corner
and saw Mr Rigby standing in the 200s. He held a
stack of books. They looked like props.

'You need anything?' he asked.

'I'm right, thanks.' I didn't want to lose track
of the shelves I'd checked.

'You still go running?' Mr Rigby asked. A couple of students wriggled past us down the aisle, heading for the beanbags.

'Yeah.' I thought he was going to tell me to be careful.

He said, 'I went to church with Robbie and his family.'

I held my breath.

Mr Rigby nodded. He tapped a finger against one of the books in his hand. 'Here.'

The book was called *Striding with a Singular Heart*. On its cover, a silhouetted woman in running shorts sped towards a marbled mountain.

'Be careful with that dust jacket. It's old.'

I'm jogging down the hill, breathing deeply, holding myself upright, and Robbie makes his way into my mind where he hangs like a teardrop. A watery breeze picks up the smell of the ocean. The endorphins are setting in and I start the timer again. I shake the blunt, numb ends of my fingers. The book Mr Rigby lent me said that some people think running is like praying. It isn't difficult to turn running into praying, or turn disbelief into faith. It isn't difficult to turn sadness or confusion into the slim white nerve of a cord looped and fixed around a beam.

Contributors

Andreas Å Andersson is a writer of fiction and poetry from Vetlanda, Sweden, currently living in Melbourne. His work has appeared in *Rabbit Poetry Journal*, *Scum Magazine* and the Emerging Writers' Festival anthology, *9 Slices*.

Gail Chrisfield works as a corporate writer and writes short fiction. She lives on Victoria's south-west coast with her partner and their two furkids. Her voluntary roles as Write Here in Surf Coast Convenor and Writers Victoria's inaugural Regional Ambassador enable her to meet and encourage other local writers.

Yvonne Edgren was born in Finland to a Swedish-speaking family and migrated to Australia when she was a child. She taught for some years in a small progressive school, and is currently enrolled in a doctorate at Western Sydney University's Writing and Society Research Centre. She is working on a novel.

Laura Elvery is a writer from Brisbane. Her work has been published in *The Big Issue Fiction Edition*, *Kill Your Darlings*, *Award Winning Australian Writing* and *Griffith Review*. In 2016, Laura was shortlisted in the Queensland Literary Awards for an unpublished manuscript by an emerging writer.

Judyth Emanuel has short stories published in *Overland Literary Magazine*, *Electric Literature Recommended Reading*, *Intrinsick*, *Fanzine*, *STORGY*, *One Page*. Her stories are forthcoming in *Literary Orphans*, *Quail Bell*, *Verity Lane*, and *PULP Literature*. She is a finalist in The Raven Short Story Contest, semi-finalist for the *Conium Review* Flash Fiction Contest and shortlisted for the Margaret River Short Story Prize. Find Judyth online at www.judythemanuel.com or on twitter @judythewrite

Else Fitzgerald is a Melbourne-based writer. Her work has appeared in various places including *Visible Ink*, *Australian Book Review*, *The Suburban Review*, *Offset* and *Award Winning Australian Writing*.

Charlotte Guest is a Western Australian writer and publishing officer at UWA Publishing. Her work has appeared in *Griffith Review*, *Overland*, *Voiceworks*, *Australian Book Review*, *The West Australian*, *Westerly* and elsewhere.

Keren Heenan has won a number of Australian short story awards, including the Alan Marshall, Southern Cross and Hal Porter awards, and she was placed second in the 2015 Fish Prize. She's been published in Australian journals and anthologies, including *Island*, *Overland*, *AWAW*, and in *Aesthetica Creative Writing Annual* (UK) 2014 and *Fish Anthology* (IRE) 2015.

John Jenkins is a widely published and much-travelled former journalist who now lives on the rural outskirts of Melbourne and writes short fiction, non-fiction, plays and poetry. He was anthologised in *Knitting and Other Stories* (MRP, 2013) and is presently putting the finishing touches on his tenth poetry collection.

Erin Courtney Kelly is a writer from Melbourne. She is a previous winner of the John Marsden Prize for Short Fiction, has been nominated for the Melbourne Lord Mayor's Creative Writing Prize and was published in *Women of Letters* (Penguin). She has been published in journals both nationally and internationally.

Marian Matta began concentrating on the short story format in 2006 after being inspired by Annie Proulx's *Brokeback Mountain* and relishing the creative freedom provided by online fan fiction. Grandmother, history tragic, Internet junkie and circus student, she lives in the hills outside Melbourne, and is pleased to call Heath Ledger her muse.

Sophie McClelland is a copy-editor from Wales who moved to Perth in 2012 after a decade in London where she attained an English degree at Kings College London and spent many happy years working for an independent publisher. She has two young children and 'Dependence Day' is her first short story.

Belinda McCormick is a Melbourne-based writer of contemporary short fiction. When not delving into the difficult emotional territory of broken things, she dabbles in the comedic world of her real-life adventure.

Jo Morrison lives in Fremantle, Western Australia. She began her writing career as a journalist before completing her creative writing PhD at Murdoch University, where she now works as a sessional tutor. Her writing has previously been published in *Westerly* and *Celebrity Studies* journal. Find Jo online at www.jodijo.com or on twitter @JodijoMo.

Emily Paull is a writer of short fiction and historical fiction. She has been a Young Writer-in-Residence at the Katherine Susannah Prichard Writers' Centre, was shortlisted for the 2015 John Marsden / Hachette Australia Prize, and was highly commended in the Hadow/Stuart award run by the Fellowship of Australian Writers, WA in 2016. Her work can be found in the *[Re]sisters* anthology and in *Shibboleth and Other Stories*, as well as on her blog—www.emilypaull.com

Leslie Thiele loves reading books and writing stories. Sometimes she gets mixed up and scribbles ideas in the margins. Her short fiction has been commended and shortlisted in various competitions, sometimes they have even won! Leslie studies writing at Bunbury's ECU campus and has learnt more there about a writers craft than she ever managed by herself.

Miriam Zolin's fiction and non fiction have appeared in *Griffith Review*, a *Sleepers Almanac*, *Australian Book Review*, *Canberra Times*, *Sydney Morning Herald* and some other places. Her first novel was *Tristessa & Lucido* (UQP, 2003). She is working on the next one. Miriam lives in Mansfield in North East Victoria.

**Other Margaret River
Short Story Competition titles**

Things that are found in trees & other stories
EDITED BY RICHARD ROSSITER

The stories in this collection 'are insightful,
sensitive stories, wide-ranging in their interests
and, I believe, deeply rewarding. In all of them,
there is "something new" for us to discover.'

– Richard Rossiter, Editor

Knitting & other stories
EDITED BY RICHARD ROSSITER

'These 24 stories continue—as fine stories
always do—to speak, to unsettle, to shine
long after you've closed the book.'

– Amanda Curtin

Trouble with flying & other stories
EDITED BY RICHARD ROSSITER
AND SUSAN MIDALIA

'These stories, the best of the 2014 Margaret River Short Story Competition, are beautiful illuminations. They deal in moments of clarity, desperation, respite, decision and grace. They deal in many voices … This book is a delight to read. It's strange and unexpected.'

– Fiona McFarlane, author of
The Night Guest and *The High Places*

Lost Boy & other stories
EDITED BY ESTELLE TANG

'Behind every situation recounted in this collection there is a story of vulnerability, and a quest for grace. Some find it only to lose it again, but there is always great courage in their pursuit.'

– Sian Prior, author of *Shy: a memoir*

Shibboleth & other stories
EDITED BY LAURIE STEED

'The volume's abundance means it is best read slowly
or intermittently to savour each story's intricacy
and craft. Margaret River Press' commitment to
showcasing Australian writers deserves support.
Editor Laurie Steed describes the "right" short
stories as ones that "sear their mark upon one's
soul". Repeatedly, this collection does that.'

– Joanne Shiells was formerly a retail book
buyer and an editor of *Books+Publishing*.

MARGARET RIVER
·PRESS·